"Who **doing in my bed?"**

Elisabeth's eyes rounded in surprise. "You don't know?"

Tim shook his head. "Nope. I haven't a clue. Not that I'm complaining, you understand. I feel honored. More than honored, actually. I feel—"

"Never mind what you feel, Tim," she interrupted, her eyes taking in his taut body and heated gaze. "I'm afraid you're getting the wrong idea."

"How could I possibly misunderstand? You're here. I'm here—"

"Do you know who you are?" Elisabeth demanded.

"You mean you don't know? Are you in the habit of sleeping with strange men?"

"Of course I know who you are! You're the one who received the blow to your head! Do you know where you are?"

Tim smiled. "In bed with you," he pointed out. "I would just like to add that I can think of nowhere else I would prefer to be at the moment. Now, then," he went on, "if that's all your questions..."

Dear Reader,

Welcome to Silhouette—experience the magic of the wonderful world where two people fall in love. Meet heroines who will make you cheer for their happiness, and heroes (be they the boy next door or a handsome, mysterious stranger) who will win your heart. Silhouette Romance reflects the magic of love—sweeping you away with books that will make you laugh and cry, heartwarming, poignant stories that will move you time and time again.

In the coming months we're publishing romances by many of your all-time favorites, such as Diana Palmer, Brittany Young, Sondra Stanford and Annette Broadrick. Your response to these authors and our other Silhouette Romance authors has served as a touchstone for us, and we're pleased to bring you more books with Silhouette's distinctive medley of charm, wit and—above all—*romance*.

I hope you enjoy this book and the many stories to come. Experience the magic!

Sincerely,

Tara Hughes
Senior Editor
Silhouette Books

ANNETTE BROADRICK

A Love Remembered

Silhouette Romance

Published by Silhouette Books New York

America's Publisher of Contemporary Romance

To my one and only sister,
Derralee...
who insisted that I tell
Tim's story

SILHOUETTE BOOKS
300 E. 42nd St., New York, N.Y. 10017

ISBN: 0-373-08676-8

First Silhouette Books printing October 1989

Printed in the U.S.A.

Books by Annette Broadrick

Silhouette Romance

Circumstantial Evidence #329
Provocative Peril #359
Sound of Summer #412
Unheavenly Angel #442
Strange Enchantment #501
Mystery Lover #533
That's What Friends Are For #544
Come Be My Love #609
A Love Remembered #676

Silhouette Christmas Stories 1988

"*Christmas Magic*"

Silhouette Desire

Hunter's Prey #185
Bachelor Father #219
Hawk's Flight #242
Deceptions #272
Choices #283
Heat of the Night #314
Made in Heaven #336
Return to Yesterday #360
Adam's Story #367
Momentary Marriage #414
With All My Heart #433
A Touch of Spring #464
Irresistible #499

ANNETTE BROADRICK

lives on the shores of The Lake of the Ozarks in Missouri where she spends her time doing what she loves most—reading and writing romantic fiction. "For twenty-five years I lived in various large cities, working as a legal secretary, a very high-stress occupation. I never thought I was capable of making a career change at this point in my life, but thanks to Silhouette I am now able to write full time in the peaceful surroundings that have turned my life into a dream come true."

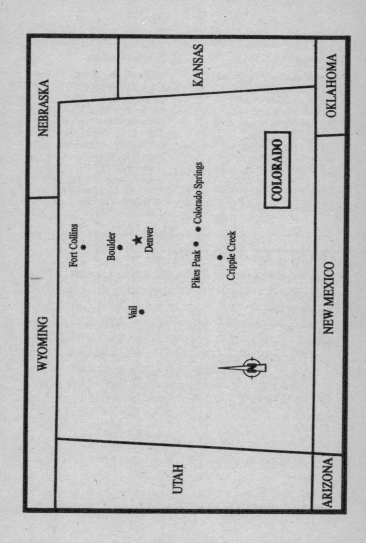

Chapter One

The first thing Tim Walker noticed when he woke up was the ferocious pounding in his head. It echoed like a steady drumbeat and created a pulsing pain that could not be ignored.

No hangover had ever felt so rough. He'd never been one to do much drinking, but he must have really tied one on this time.

He groaned, groping for his head in a useless attempt to stop the ceaseless drumbeat.

Tim received his first shock when a soft voice spoke from somewhere nearby. He froze, his hand halfway to his head.

"Are you in pain? Let me get your medication for you."

His eyes flew open. A light came on, and he used his hand to shield his eyes from the glare. He watched warily as a woman slipped from beside him in the bed and disappeared through a doorway nearby.

What the hell? he wondered, forcing his eyes to stay open despite the light. Who was she, and what was she doing in his bed?

Tim's second shock came when he discovered that he was not, in fact, in his room at all. He looked around, his sense of bewilderment growing. Was he dreaming? Or had something in the universe slipped a cog and had he somehow awakened in another time?

The room could have come from the nineteenth century or before. The bed in which he lay was a four-poster with a canopy. Draperies hung at each corner. Across the room was a massive fireplace, and grouped in front of it were two wing chairs and a table. Heavy drapes framed windows that were tall and narrow, ending only a few inches from the floor.

He closed his eyes deliberately, deciding that he was dreaming, even though he couldn't understand the significance of the dream.

Being single, he certainly wasn't used to waking up to find a woman in bed with him. At the moment he wasn't even dating anyone. Perhaps his lack of a love life had prompted him to dream about a woman, but why the room?

Slowly Tim opened his eyes. The room hadn't changed.

Where the hell was he?

He heard a sound and looked around. The woman was back.

"Here, these should help." Her voice was a rich contralto that caused a tingling in his spine as though she had run her fingers lightly across it.

She sat on the bed beside him and held out two white tablets and a glass filled with water. Now that the lamplight fell across her features he could see her more clearly.

He had never seen this woman before in his life. Without a doubt, he would have remembered.

Her silver blond hair shone in the soft light, falling around her shoulders and down her back in a profusion of waves. Green eyes, slightly tilted like a cat's, stared at him from behind a fringe of impossibly long dark lashes, their color a stark contrast to her hair.

High cheekbones created a classically shaped face, and yet it was her mouth that drew his attention. Her upper lip curved enticingly above a full lower lip that gave her mouth a slightly pouty look.

His gaze slowly lowered to take in the powder-blue silk and lace of her gown, lingering at the V between her breasts and finally coming to a stop at her hands, which held the glass and pills.

Tim stared at the pills with suspicion. "What are they?"

Her brows lifted slightly. "The pain medication Dr. Madison prescribed. Don't you remember?"

Of course he didn't remember, damn it! He didn't remember much of anything at the moment, except the pain in his head. Tim decided that he wasn't going to admit his memory lapse. Not at the moment, at least. No doubt it was temporary, and he'd wake up in the morning and they would laugh about it.

He hoped.

At the moment he didn't really care about much of anything. The pain seemed to be intensifying, and his head felt as though it was going to explode momentarily.

He held out his hand, and she dropped the tablets into his palm. Quickly tossing them into his mouth, he drank the water and slowly returned his head to the pillow, laying his arm across his eyes to shade them.

"Thanks," he muttered.

"You're welcome." Her voice held a faint trace of amusement, as though their formality in the middle of the night and in such an intimate situation teased her sense of humor.

If his head wasn't pounding so, no doubt he could better enjoy the joke. At the moment, Tim found nothing amusing.

He heard the small click of the light switch and allowed his arm to fall away from his head. Inky darkness greeted him. The mattress shifted, and he knew that the unknown woman was once again sharing his bed.

Tim continued to lie there staring into the darkness as he waited for relief from the pain. He let his mind wander in hopes of finding a stray answer or two to the situation. He didn't know where he was or why, nor did he know the lady who so calmly and intimately shared his bed.

What did he know?

His name was Timothy Joseph Walker. He lived in Denver, Colorado, and worked wherever he happened to be sent.

His work for the government was never defined. His name was not on any payroll, nor was his job description printed in any manual. Only a handful of people knew who he was and what he did. He thought of himself as a person who gathered information and at times utilized his negotiating skills.

Tim knew that he was good at what he did. He also knew that he was tired of his life-style, the lack of permanence and the danger inherent in what he did.

What was his last memory?

His mind seemed to blank out at the question.

He could come up with no explanation for what he was doing in a strange bedroom nursing a violent headache with a beautiful woman he'd never seen before playing nurturing angel. Whimsically he wondered if he had offered his headache as an excuse to the woman earlier in the evening.

Waking up in a stranger's bedroom was not typical behavior for him. So what was going on?

The pounding in his head began to ease, and he took a deep breath, allowing the air in his lungs to escape in a soft sigh.

The woman spoke in her soft, husky voice. "Is the pain easing any?"

She must be tuned to every sound he made, he decided with a sense of strain. "Some."

"You'll probably feel much better by tomorrow. I hope the doctor knew what he was talking about when he called your concussion a mild one."

Cloudlike fog seemed to roll through his head, causing him to drift away from the sound of her voice. He could smell the light floral perfume she wore.

Searching through the whirling fog within his head, he finally found words to respond.

"I appreciate your concern."

Her hand brushed his shoulder, then slid along his cheekbone. Once again he heard the slight sound of amusement in her voice. "Try to rest," she whispered.

He smiled, warmed by her touch. His last waking thought was to reflect that if this was a dream he certainly had great taste in fantasy women!

The next time Tim awakened, sunlight poured through the windows across the room. He blinked from the light and took careful inventory of the pain in his head before he did something foolish—like moving. He noted that the pain had lost some of its urgency but he was fairly certain that he would be well advised not to leap out of bed and start touching his toes.

Shifting slowly, he rolled onto his back and found himself staring into the top of the canopied bed. He hadn't dreamed the place after all.

Now that his head was clearer, Tim tried to search for answers. What had the woman said last night? Something about a concussion. Was that why he couldn't remember anything?

What could have happened to him?

He felt the bed shift, and he turned his head faster than he wished he had. Forcing himself to move more cautiously, Tim came up on his elbow and stared at the woman who slept beside him, curled up on her side, facing him.

Her long hair was draped across her shoulders and curled around her hand, which rested on the pillow. Her dark lashes brushed against softly tinted cheeks that looked like satin. The covers rested around her hips, showing him the curving line from her shoulders down to a narrow waist and widening slightly down to the covers.

Tim decided that he must have awakened in the middle of a fairy tale. He had found Sleeping Beauty.

He watched with a great deal of interest as she stirred once again, realizing that she must have moved earlier thereby awakening him. She rolled onto her back, her eyelids slowly opening to reveal her sleepy green gaze.

She blinked uncertainly when their eyes met.

Tim could feel himself responding to her deliciously disheveled appearance. He became aware of the heavy beat of his heart as his blood began to surge throughout his body.

"I must have done something right in my life," he mused aloud, "to be rewarded in such a manner. I just wish I knew what it was, and I would concentrate on continuing to do it."

"What are you talking about?" she managed to say, despite a rather delicate—almost kittenlike—yawn.

"Who are you and what are you doing in my bed?" was his warm response.

Her startled reaction removed much of the sultry, sleepy look about her eyes. They rounded in surprise.

"You don't know?"

He shook his head. "Nope. I haven't a clue."

She raised her head slightly, staring into his eyes intently. "Oh, no." She closed her eyes and shook her head, a rather pained expression on her face.

"Not that I'm complaining, you understand." He immediately sought to reassure her. "I feel honored. More than honored, actually. I feel—"

"Never mind what you feel, Tim," she interrupted, her eyes scanning his taut body and heated gaze. "I'm afraid you're getting the wrong idea."

He glanced around the room as though searching for some explanation from the drapes or furniture, then looked at her with a grin. "How could I possibly misunderstand? What is there to misunderstand? You are here. I am here. You are a beautiful woman. I am very appreciative of all your charms. In fact, I'm—"

She sat up, inching away from him. "Yes, I'm very aware of what you are. You are concussed. You're not yourself." She imitated his all-encompassing glance around the room and added, almost to herself, "And I'm in trouble."

He reached out and cupped her bare shoulder soothingly. "Not at all. I'm perfectly harmless, you know. I wouldn't take advantage of you, not unless you encouraged me, of course." He peered at her hopefully. "You *are* encouraging me, aren't you?"

Despite her obvious effort to control it, she laughed. "If I didn't know better, I'd swear you were drunk," she admitted ruefully.

"Drunk on your charms," he agreed with a grin.

"What is my name?" she asked in a stern voice.

Tim blinked. He thought for a moment, then shrugged. "What's in a name, after all? A rose by any other name would still smell as sweet."

She touched her forehead lightly with the tips of her fingers where a slight frown was forming. "Isn't it a little early in the day for quoting poetry?"

Tim glanced at her in surprise. "Is that what I'm doing? You mean that wasn't original?"

She shook her head.

"But it was sincere," he pointed out.

"Do you remember anything?" She could not quite hide the concern in her voice.

"About what?" A reasonable enough request, he thought, for clarification this early in the day.

"Do you know who you are?"

"Of course I do."

"Tell me."

He looked at her suspiciously. "You mean you don't know? Are you in the habit of sleeping with strange men? I should warn you that such a habit could be quite lethal."

"Of course I know who you are! Don't be ridiculous. You're the one that received the blow to the head!" She pushed her hair over her shoulder in exasperation and glared at him.

One long strand of hair continued to lie across the upper curve of her breast. With delicate precision Tim lifted the curl with his index finger and carefully moved his hand until the curl slid behind her shoulder. He glanced at her and smiled, feeling pleased with his helpful assistance.

She sighed and looked away from him.

He studied her profile, intrigued with the view of her small, patrician nose and the way her short upper lip revealed the pouting curve of her lower one. There was a great deal of determination exhibited in the lift of her small chin. He found himself itching to trace the line of her jaw, the slender arch of her neck, the slope of her shoulders, the—

"Tim Walker," he finally said out loud in an effort to distract his thoughts.

She looked around at him, her eyes registering her relief. "Oh, thank God!"

"For what?"

"You remember something."

He shrugged modestly.

"Do you know where you are?"

He smiled. "In bed with you," he pointed out. "I would just like to add that I can think of nowhere else I would prefer to be at the moment. Now, then," he went on, slipping his arm around her and tugging her toward him, "if that's all your questions, we can—"

He had caught her off balance, and she fell across him, causing him to land flat on his back once more. He winced and absently rubbed his head. Obviously he wasn't in as good shape as he could hope to be given the circumstances.

She pushed against his shoulders a little more forcefully than he considered necessary and drew away from him.

"Do you always come across so aggressively to women whose names you don't even know?" she asked sweetly.

His last move definitely had been a mistake. The sleeping drummers in his head had come awake with a vengeance, and the cadence of their beat pounded rhythmically along the lining of his skull.

"Only when I find them in my bed," he managed to reply, wishing she would lower her voice. He closed his eyes.

She was silent as though aware of his unvoiced wish.

Tim wished to hell he knew what was going on. Whatever had happened to him had certainly managed to incapacitate him on several levels, only one of which had to do with his memory.

"So who are you?" he finally repeated after the silence had stretched between them for several minutes.

"My name is Elisabeth Barringer—"

"Barringer?" He opened his eyes in surprise. "Are you any kin to Charles Winston Barringer?"

Her eyebrows lifted slightly. "So. At least you remember my grandfather." She nodded, looking almost relieved.

Tim felt anything but relieved. "I just spent the night with Charlie's granddaughter? Dear God, he's going to kill me." *If my head doesn't explode and wipe me out first,* he added silently.

As though she were talking to a child, Tim decided resentfully, Elisabeth continued. "What do you remember about my grandfather?"

Tim forced himself to concentrate, willing the pain to subside. "I met Charlie several years ago, when he was still in Washington, D.C. We became friends. After he retired we stayed in touch. We both had homes in Colorado...we had several things in common...." Tim opened his eyes. "I don't remember his ever mentioning having a granddaughter."

"Was there any reason he should?"

Tim considered the question for a few minutes, feeling as though his brain was made up of several cogs of machinery that had been drenched in molasses and refused to move with any degree of briskness.

"No," he finally admitted. "I suppose not."

"Do you remember my grandfather's letter?"

Letter? Tim tried to think. He remembered the pile of mail that generally awaited him at the post office when he returned home after weeks away. What could he recall? A letter from Charlie? When? About what?

In disgust he shook his head, then wished he hadn't. He groaned.

"Your head is bothering you, isn't it?"

He opened his eyes, absently noting that the light seemed to create even more pain. He squinted, looking at her. "You must be psychic."

She rolled her eyes. "And you are definitely being sarcastic."

Elisabeth tossed the covers back and climbed out of bed. In the daylight Tim could see that the bed was on some sort of platform. What the hell? Did Charlie treat his granddaughter like some damned princess? What was Charlie going to do when he discovered that the princess hadn't slept alone? It was one thing to find her sleeping. It was another to be spending the night sleeping beside her.

Maybe Charlie would listen to reason. Tim would explain about his hangover—no, she had called it a concussion. Even better. A concussion was not something one did to oneself, after all. He was concussed. He wasn't of sound mind. He'd be honest and explain that he didn't know how the hell he'd wound up in Princess Elisabeth's bed but it was all very innocent. He was in no condition for it to be anything else but innocent.

Perhaps he needn't go quite *that* far in his explanation. Now that he knew who she was, Tim would certainly make sure that he kept his hands off her.

Charlie had written him a letter? Why? Tim couldn't remember the last time he had visited Cripple Creek. He'd been in the habit of dropping in on his old friend when he had a free moment, but there never seemed much spare time in Tim's life.

Was that where they were now? It made sense, even though he'd never been through all the rooms of the hundred-year-old mansion that was Charlie's pride and joy. Certainly the downstairs area had been furnished in keeping with its period. Or perhaps Elisabeth had chosen to decorate her room in such a manner. He had a sinking hunch that he was, in fact, in Elisabeth Barringer's bedroom.

"Here." Her voice, although as low and vibrant as ever, had a distinctly schoolmarmish tone. He forced his eyes open. Gone was the blue-gowned nymph he had seen earlier. In her place stood a young woman dressed in a lightweight pink sweater and well-worn jeans. A single thick braid was draped over one shoulder. She held out a glass to him, and two white tablets.

He had no trouble remembering her doing this sometime during the night. He looked at the tablets with suspicion.

"Go on, take them. They'll help your headache."

"They knock me out," he pointed out.

"Not really. What they do is ease the pain and you relax, which causes you to sleep better."

"From the looks of things, I seem to be the one who slept for a hundred years."

"What are you talking about?"

He forced himself to sit up. "I need to know what's going on. I need some answers."

"There's nothing you can do at the moment, anyway, Tim," she pointed out. "You should rest and give your head time to heal. Perhaps then you'll be able to think a little more clearly."

"That's easy for you to say. You're not the one with a memory problem."

"Yes, I know. At the moment I remember a great deal more than I wish I did!"

Reluctantly he reached out and took the tablets and the glass of water from her.

"What do you mean by that remark?"

She shook her head.

Tim knew that whether or not he liked the idea, he needed relief from the pain that seemed to be steadily growing in his head. Although he needed answers, at the moment he wouldn't be able to do much with them. After swallowing the tablets he drained the glass and handed it to her.

"Is your grandfather here?"

Her calm expression wavered as a flash of pain swept over her face. "No."

"Where is he?"

"He's in the hospital."

"My God! What's wrong with him?"

She shook her head, looking through the windows without speaking. She swallowed as though she found the simple action difficult. Tim caught a brief sign of moisture in the corner of her eye, but when she turned and faced him, her expression was calm once more.

"He's dying."

Chapter Two

Dying? What happened?"

Elisabeth moved away from the side of the bed, starting down the steps of the platform. "His heart is tired."

Tim lowered himself to his pillow once again. Charlie Barringer dying? It didn't seem possible. Charlie had always appeared to be ageless, his strength and stamina such an integral part of him that Tim couldn't imagine Charlie ever succumbing to old age.

"Is that why he wrote me?"

Elisabeth continued across the room toward the door. "Among other things." She didn't sound pleased with whatever other things might have caused her grandfather to write.

"I need to see him," Tim muttered.

"You're in no shape to go anywhere," she replied in a reasonable tone of voice that Tim found more than a little irritating. He hated it when someone pointed out the obvious to him.

What wasn't obvious was why he was sleeping with her. What wasn't obvious was the reason Charlie had written to him. What wasn't obvious was how he'd come to be recovering from a concussion.

He noticed that she wasn't rushing to answer any of those questions.

Tim could feel the soothing relief from pain reaching into his head like cool fingers caressing the ache away. He had no choice but to allow the blissful fog of oblivion to overtake him one more time.

But he would have his answers. Oh, yes, indeed. He was used to being in control . . . of his life and his environment. He liked having his own way.

No doubt that was why he had never married. Marriage was made up of compromise. He'd been on his own for too many years. Besides, he had never met any woman who had tempted him to consider settling down . . . no one at all.

He carried the steady green-eyed gaze of the woman who had shared his bed into sleep with him.

From the position of the sun when he awakened, he knew several hours had passed. However, his head felt considerably more clear and Tim's first thought was of Charlie. He had to see him. Somehow he knew that Charlie was the key to at least some of the mystery that surrounded Tim at the moment.

With grim determination Tim crawled out of bed, descending the ridiculous steps and searching for the bathroom. After a long, hot shower he felt even better. The only thing that unnerved him was to find his shaving gear in the bathroom cabinet. He had certainly made himself at home, he decided, cringing at the thought. Whatever could he have been thinking of?

After shaving he returned to the bedroom, looking for his clothes. As soon as he opened the closet door he spotted one of his shirts hanging there. He shook his head and reached for it. A pair of his slacks hung nearby.

Glancing around, he spotted a chest of drawers and decided to see if he would find any of his socks and underwear. Why wasn't he more surprised to discover both in the second drawer?

Somehow he had a hunch that his moving in with Charlie's granddaughter had not been Charlie's idea, and Tim had trouble believing he, himself, would have suggested it.

That left the princess.

As soon as he was dressed Tim opened the door that led into the hallway. Spotting the top of the stairs, he headed toward them. By the time he was halfway down he saw a familiar face—Charlie's housekeeper.

"Hello, Mrs. Brodie." He paused at the bottom of the stairs.

The short, middle-aged woman had been crossing the wide foyer when he spoke, and she glanced up, obviously surprised at the unexpected voice.

"Mr. Walker! You shouldn't be out of bed!"

Wonderful. Did everyone know where he'd been sleeping?

"I'm feeling much better, actually. I was hoping I could find something to eat."

Her face lit up. "Now, that I can help you with. I have everything ready on a tray for you. If you'd like to follow me into the kitchen."

He dropped his arm around her shoulders and hugged her. "With your skill in the kitchen, my dear lady, I would follow you anywhere."

She laughed, her cheeks glowing a fiery hue.

"Where's Elisabeth?" he asked, watching her bustling around heating something in the microwave and pouring him a cup of coffee.

"She's at the hospital. She hoped to get back before you woke up."

"Is there any word on Charlie's condition?"

Mrs. Brodie motioned for him to have a seat, and he followed her silent instructions. "At the moment the doctors say he's holding his own." She shook her head. "There's just so little they can do for him."

"Elisabeth said it's his heart."

"Yes. It's just a question of time, I'm afraid."

"How long has he been in the hospital?"

"But don't you remember? You arrived a few days after he was admitted."

Tim shook his head. "I'm afraid not. That knock on the head seems to have completely wiped away my recent memories."

Her eyes rounded. "You don't say!"

"Yes. Unfortunately."

"Does Elisabeth know?"

"I suppose." He remembered their early morning discussion. "Yes, I'm sure she does."

"Oh, that's awful, really awful. Do you think the doctors will be able to do something for you?"

"I don't think anyone will be able to do anything about it. Head injuries are tricky. I've been around more of them than I would have liked. Fortunately, even those that have caused amnesia have generally not been permanent."

Tim was pleased to hear himself sound so casual, so unconcerned. He only wished he believed all that he was saying.

There was no guarantee that his memory would return. None whatsoever. Even if there was, he didn't want to sit around and wait for it to happen. Patience had never been one of his virtues. He wanted some answers. He wanted them now.

As soon as he finished eating, he announced, "I'm going in to town to see Charlie."

Mrs. Brodie had been busy chopping vegetables and preparing a roast for dinner. She glanced up at him in surprise. "Oh, but, Mr. Walker, do you think you should be doing so much?"

"It won't hurt me. I feel much better than I did when I first woke up this morning."

Tim left the kitchen and let himself out the front door, glad he had worn his sport jacket. Even in May, the late afternoon felt cool to him, and he knew the night would be even cooler.

Okay, so perhaps he was rushing things a little. He had to admit that he had felt considerably better at other times in his life than he did right then, but he wasn't going to curl up into a fetal position and suck his thumb. Maybe later, he decided with a grin, climbing into his car.

Strange that he couldn't remember driving here, although he'd visited Charlie at the house several times. He knew his way into town without thought. He watched for the sign along the highway that signaled the correct exit for the local hospital.

The last hospital he'd been in was in St. Louis when his friend Gregory Duncan had been recuperating from a gunshot wound. That had been several years ago, right after Greg and Brandi were married.

That was one relationship that gave Tim reason to believe that with some people, marriage was the best thing that could happen. He had known both of them for years before they had met each other. He felt a special closeness with each of them. As for their children, he couldn't feel closer to his own than he did to the Duncan tots.

He loved those kids, partly because he knew they were the closest he would ever come to having a family of his own. He had accepted that idea years ago. In his business there was no way a man could plan a future of any sort.

He followed the street signs to the hospital and pulled into the designated parking area. Tim wondered if Elisabeth would still be there or whether they had passed on the highway. He had no idea what sort of car she drove.

He knew nothing about her, but for some reason he couldn't keep his mind off her.

After stopping at the front desk to find out Charlie's room number, Tim followed the arrows until he saw the door, which was ajar. He pushed on it until he could step inside the room.

Elisabeth stood beside the hospital bed, her hand engulfed by the larger one of the man who was lying propped up in the bed. He was a big man, with a mane of white hair and bushy white brows that he could use to good advantage when he felt it necessary to intimidate someone. He turned his head at the sound of the door opening, a look of surprise on his face.

Tim felt the shock of seeing Charlie. His color was poor, his cheeks appeared sunken, but his eyes still glittered with sharp intelligence. No one had to tell Tim how Charlie was doing. Not now.

"What the hell are you doing here, boy? You're supposed to be in bed."

"Says who?" Tim's mild manner hid his concern.

"The doctors, that's who!" Although the delivery was in keeping with the man Tim knew, his voice was weak.

"Do you do everything the doctors tell you?" Tim asked with amused interest.

"We're not talking about me."

Tim glanced over at Elisabeth and noticed that she would not meet his eyes. He wondered why. Could it be that she was afraid he might tell Charlie where he had spent the night?

"Good evening, Elisabeth," he said, smiling politely.

She glanced at Charlie, then looked slightly past Tim.

"Good evening."

"Elisabeth tells me you're suffering from a memory lapse," Charlie said after a rather awkward silence.

Tim shrugged. "I'm afraid so."

"You don't have any idea what you're doing here in Cripple Creek, then, do you?"

"Not a clue. I was hoping you could fill me in. I have a hunch it has something to do with a letter you wrote."

"Ah. So you remember that."

Tim shook his head. "Elisabeth mentioned it. Unfortunately, I can't recall it at all."

"I see," the older man said, looking at the woman who still held his hand.

She met his gaze with a level one of her own, but Tim noticed that her chin was raised and her jaw was tense.

Charlie looked at Tim. "I suppose it's only natural that you might have some questions."

Elisabeth spoke up. "But you aren't the one to give him the answers, Granddad. You need your rest."

"Nonsense. I've got all of eternity waiting with nothing to do but rest. I'm not going to my grave without trying to take care of this situation."

Elisabeth looked at him. "If you would just follow the doctors' directions, you'd probably be able to go home in a few days."

"Like hell," the old man muttered.

"Elisabeth's right, Charlie. Why don't you try to rest? I can come back tomorrow. We'll visit then."

"You're here now. I may not be here tomorrow." Charlie patted Elisabeth's hand. "I want you to go home now, honey. You've been here all afternoon. Tim and I need to talk.''

''But, Granddad—''

''Don't argue with me. You know it will just upset me.''

She choked on a laugh. ''You're disgraceful, you know that, don't you? Using your health as a weapon against me.''

''Never against you, love. Just using whatever tools I have at my disposal to get my own way. What's wrong with that?''

Elisabeth shook her head, knowing she was defeated. She looked at Tim with a silent plea, meeting his gaze for the first time since he'd walked in.

Tim found himself reassuring her. ''I'll only stay a few minutes.''

She leaned over and kissed Charlie's cheek. ''I love you, Granddad.''

''I love you, too, darlin'. Never forget that. Everything I've done has always been with your best interests in mind.''

''I know that. It's just that you and I have different ideas about what my best interests are.''

''I know it's not going to be easy for you, girl. I wish I could be there to make it easier. I've done everything I can.''

Elisabeth blinked away the moisture that seemed to fill her eyes. ''Take care of yourself. I'll see you in the morning.''

She turned away and walked out of the room without looking at Tim.

He watched the man on the bed carefully, wondering if he should, in fact, postpone their discussion.

"See this little box?" Charlie asked, pointing to what looked like a small tape recorder on his chest. "Know what it is?"

Tim shook his head.

"It's hooked up to the nurses' station down the hall. If my heart starts doing the two-step, or do-si-doin' around, they all come running—doctors, nurses—you never saw such a crowd."

"I'm sorry about your health, Charlie. You've had me convinced that nothing would ever stop you."

Charlie's smile was amused. "Yeah, well. Things happen. And life has to go on. I can't really complain. I've always enjoyed life. I've been determined to live it to the fullest. I don't have regrets. Just remember that, son." He paused, his gaze slowly taking in the room. "I insisted they leave me here because I know that my old ticker isn't going to work much longer. I didn't want Elisabeth wearing herself out looking after me."

"From what I've observed since I woke up this morning, she's been too busy looking after me."

Charlie grinned. "And you don't have any idea why. She's been mighty upset over that, let me tell you."

"Because I can't remember anything?"

"Partly. Partly because she didn't care about all the arrangements you and I have made these past few weeks. The only way I could get her to agree to them was to play on her sympathy."

There was so much said that Tim didn't understand, that he didn't know where to start. "I've been here weeks?"

"Something like a month, maybe."

It was worse than he thought. How could a whole month be missing from his life, possibly more? "You'd better fill me in, Charlie."

"Yes. It feels a little strange, going through all of it with you once more. It was tough enough the first time. Sometimes I wonder why God ever intended us to have family."

"You mean Elisabeth?"

"Hell, no, I don't mean Elisabeth. She's the only thing that's been worth anything to me. Has been for years."

"How come you never told me about her?"

Charlie sighed. "Don't really know, Tim. For one thing, she's only moved in with me these last couple of years, and you and I have been out of touch lately." He frowned. "Besides, I have to admit that I've been ashamed of the way she's been treated by all of us . . . like some orphaned stepchild."

Tim didn't want to interrupt Charlie, but he hated to see him wear himself out. And Tim needed some answers.

"Why did you write me, Charlie?"

The older man's eyes closed for a moment, as though gathering strength. "I wrote when I got the verdict about my heart. I managed to pull through a massive heart attack, but there's not much they can do for me without surgery. And I'm too old for surgery.

Hell, I'll be eighty-two if I live to see my next birthday."

Tim shook his head. "I had no idea. I thought you were in your sixties."

"Humph. I've got grandsons pushing forty—Jason's thirty-eight and Marcus is a couple of years younger. Elisabeth's brothers," he muttered with evident distaste.

"She doesn't look that old."

"Of course she doesn't. She's not quite thirty. And she's nothing like them, thank God. Maybe that's because they have different mothers."

"I see."

"The hell you do. I know I'm not making much sense. My son, Chuck, never got around to divorcing his first wife before he moved in with Elisabeth's mother. He was killed overseas before he ever knew she was pregnant with Elisabeth. I never met Cathy. I have a feeling I would have enjoyed her. I always hoped that she made the last couple years of Chuck's life happy."

Tim had heard the story of Charlie's only child, had sat with him one night as he'd relived the loss of his son, but had never discussed the children the son had left behind.

"How did you find out about Elisabeth?"

"Her mother had left a letter with her lawyer, to be mailed to me only in the event something happened to her before Elisabeth was grown. So I didn't meet Elisabeth until she was a teenager. But I knew she was mine. There was no denying her. She's the feminine version of Chuck, all right, right down to her damned stubbornness and her willfulness.''

Tim grinned. ''She couldn't have gotten any of that from you, of course.''

''Damn right. I've still got all of mine.''

The two men smiled at each other.

Charlie sighed. ''I did what I could. She was so damned full of pride. Didn't want anyone's help. Was convinced she could do everything on her own. But she was only fourteen, just going into high school.'' He shook his head. ''We went round and round. I wasn't about to be bested by some slip of a girl, though.''

''I'm sure you weren't,'' Tim murmured.

''I adopted her, you see. I had the letter from her mother. I got a copy of her birth certificate. I insisted she come live with me.''

''Did she?''

''Hell, no. We finally compromised. I convinced her the only way she could be truly independent in this world was to get the best education money could buy. And I had the money to pay for it. Finally we agreed that she would go back East to private schools, with her keeping a record of every damn dime I spent so she could pay me back.'' He chuckled. ''Damn if she didn't do that very thing!''

Tim sat forward, startled. ''How could she do that?''

''Out of sheer, unadulterated bullheadedness. She worked part time when she got a little older, and began to write on the side. Soon she started selling her work, and found a ready market.''

"What does she write?"

"Damned if I know. She seldom shows me anything. I've seen a few articles in magazines, a couple of short stories."

"They must have paid well."

"Actually, I think she sold a book once, some historical journal or treatise. Hell, I don't know. But she managed to get a nice advance. Wouldn't keep a damned dime of it, of course. Wrote me out a check while she was still in school." He shook his head, his eyes lit with pride and admiration.

"You love her very much."

"Better than I've ever loved anyone. One of the reasons I was willing to spend so many years in Washington was so I could be close to her. Used to visit her all the time. Never missed a chance to see her." He closed his eyes. "Yes, sir. We've had some real good times together." His eyes opened. "And some real shouting matches. Lord, that woman's stubborn."

"So how did you get her to move to Colorado?"

"You know, that's a funny thing. She'd already told me that she was content living back East. Had no desire to come to these parts. I had to accept that. Had no choice. I flew East one time after I retired to visit with her. We'd gone out for dinner, like always. I guess I didn't have much to say. I'd really been missing her, even though it felt good to be home." He was quiet for several moments, as though reliving a memory. "Don't know what happened, really. I still feel foolish even thinking about it. I was sitting there listening to her, thinking about how beautiful she was, how proud of her I was, and damn if I didn't start leaking tears all over the place. Damned things kept trickling down my face like sweat on a hot summer day.''

He shook his head. ''Shocked the hell out of both of us, let me tell you. Elisabeth wanted to know what was wrong, and all I could say was, 'I miss you, girl. I miss you so much.' ''

''Emotional blackmail,'' Tim said with a smile.

Charlie grinned. ''It worked. Damned if it didn't. She packed up and moved out here. Been with me ever since.''

''You're shameless, Charlie. Totally unscrupulous.''

''Well, I have to admit I like getting my own way,'' he pointed out in a modest tone of voice.

Tim began to laugh, then touched his head gingerly.

''Head still ache?''

''Some.'' He stood up. ''I need to go and you need to get some rest, Charlie.''

''Sit down, sit down. That's all I do is rest. Guess I got sidetracked a little, and there's still things you need to know.''

Reluctantly, Tim sank into the chair and folded his arms. He would keep the old man on track this time and try not to let him wander. Tim's head was beginning to gain his attention, and he knew he was far from recovered from the mysterious injury he'd received.

''Jason and Marcus are a couple of conniving jackals determined to get their hands on every bit of property they think should be theirs.''

''Such as your place in Colorado?''

"Everything. They resent Elisabeth's presence in my life. I had to do a great deal of cover-up work in order to convince them that their father was, in fact, married to her mother when I first found out about the alliance. Otherwise they would have made her life even more miserable."

"Does she know the truth?"

"Who knows? She's always insisted it never mattered to her one way or the other. She was still who she was and that had nothing to do with whether or not her parents were married."

"Good point."

"Anyway, Jason and Marcus inherited a great deal of money and property from Chuck and from their mother, Nancy, when she died a few years ago. Nancy's from an old, prestigious family with lots of clout in all the right circles. They fit right in." He muttered something under his breath about snobs.

"So you think they're going to give Elisabeth a bad time once you're gone?"

Charlie smiled a sharkish smile that reminded Tim of who he was talking to. "They're going to try." He shifted restlessly in the bed. "But I want her to have the homestead. It means something to her. It means nothing to them. Of course the only time I tried to broach the subject she refused to discuss it with me. Said she would just give it to Jason and Marcus if they wanted it, anyway."

"Will she?"

"Of course not. She loves this place. It's the only place she truly feels at home. She was raised on a ranch, loves horses, loves the outdoors. I've watched her blossom since she's been here.''

"Being around you may have helped."

Charlie sobered. "I'd like to think so. She's given me so much. I'd like to think I've given some of that back."

Tim studied his friend for several moments in silence. "All right, Charlie, where do I come in with regard to all of this?"

When he saw the shark smile he knew he was in trouble.

"Well, at first I wasn't really sure. I wrote you because I needed to share with you some of my concerns about everything. I just needed to talk to somebody I could trust."

Tim felt a lump form in his throat and hoped he didn't disgrace himself with his own reaction to his friend's obvious sincerity.

"Thank you," Tim managed to say, "for your trust."

"Well, hell, man. If those big shots in the government trust you, why the hell shouldn't I?"

Tim smiled, shaking his head. There was only one Charlie Barringer. He was unique.

"I explained to you my concerns. At the moment Jason and Marcus are hovering like a pair of vultures, waiting to dive in and grab everything."

"Do they know you've left this property to Elisabeth?"

"Of course not."

"Are they going to contest the will?"

"They can damned well try, for all the good it'll do them. What's the point of having money if you can't pay for the best legal counsel around?"

"So there's really nothing you expect from me?" Tim felt as though a weight had been lifted from his shoulders at the thought.

"Well, at the time I wrote you the letter I was sort of hoping you'd be willing to look after Elisabeth, maybe. Give her somebody to lean on."

Tim smiled. "She doesn't appear to be a leaning kind of person."

"Don't let that damned pride of hers fool you. She's got a heart as big as the whole outdoors. Get past the prickly exterior and she's as soft and as sweet as a melting marshmallow."

Tim remembered the night before, waking up to find himself in her bed. My God, if Charlie had any idea that Tim had slept with Elisabeth, he'd permanently remove that portion of Tim's anatomy that could do possible injury to her. Tim broke out in a cold sweat at the thought.

"Maybe so, Charlie, but from everything I've observed since I woke up this morning, Elisabeth doesn't seem particularly enamored of me or my presence here."

"You don't understand, Tim. It came as quite a shock to Elisabeth to discover that you didn't recognize her."

"It was every bit as much a shock to me, let me tell you," Tim admitted.

"I'll never forget the day you first saw her," Charlie said in a reminiscent tone, as though it had been years ago rather than the few weeks that Tim knew it to be. "You seemed to almost be knocked to your knees when she walked in the door."

Tim nodded. "I can understand that. She's a beautiful woman."

"Yeah, she is, both inside and out. You looked like you were in shock. It was all I could do to keep from laughing."

Tim squirmed in his chair. "I'm glad I managed to keep you so amused."

"You had a lot of questions about her. Seemed to absorb every drop of information, much like you've done tonight, as a matter of fact."

Tim straightened. "Wait a minute, Charlie. I'm just trying to get to the bottom of all this, trying to find some explanations for what I'm doing here and why I can't remember anything."

Charlie sighed. "Well, as for the blow on your head, I'm afraid nobody seems to know much about that. You'd gone riding a few days ago, but you didn't bother telling anybody where you were going, not even Elisabeth." He grinned as though he found that amusing.

Why the hell would Charlie think Tim would tell Elisabeth if he decided to take a ride? Tim wondered.

"All I know is what I was told. Nobody wanted me upset, of course," Charlie's tone was filled with irony. "It seems your horse returned alone. Elisabeth had the presence of mind to get my hunting dogs out, gave them one of your shirts and went looking for you."

"Obviously they found me," Tim said stiffly, feeling like a fool not to remember any of this. It was as though he was listening to a story about someone else.

"Yes. You were still unconscious. No one knows what happened. There were trees in the area, and Elisabeth suggested you may have ridden under a limb and got knocked off."

Tim looked startled.

"I know," Charlie added with a grin. "I didn't bother to tell her that you've been riding since before she was born."

"Well, maybe not quite that long," Tim muttered.

"No, I decided that the less she had to worry about, the better." He frowned. "But I was really disappointed when she told me today that you had no memory of what could have happened."

"How long ago did this happen?"

"About three days ago."

"And I've been unconscious ever since? Why wasn't I taken to the hospital?"

"Oh, you regained consciousness enough to insist you were all right and didn't need to be hospitalized. Elisabeth agreed, although the doctor's been out to see you every day to make sure you were progressing normally. She wanted you there so she could look after you."

Elisabeth's concern puzzled him, unless it was because she understood the close friendship the two men shared. He would probably never understand her. As far as that went, there was no reason for him to try. Once he left here, there would be no reason for him to see her again. Tim was surprised to find the thought didn't particularly console him.

"You think I might have stumbled across something I wasn't supposed to?"

"There's that strong possibility."

"Hmm."

"Now you're beginning to see why I'm glad you decided to come see me in answer to my letter . . . then decided to stay."

Tim had been thinking about all they had discussed and looked up suddenly at Charlie's last remark. "Well, of course I'll stay for a while, Charlie. You know I wouldn't leave as long as you or Elisabeth might need me, although I don't see what I can do to help her. She may have to face some unpleasantness for a while after you're gone. But as far as I can see, that can't be helped."

"Yeah, that's the way I was looking at things when you first arrived, Tim. I couldn't see any way to protect Elisabeth from what the future might bring. That's why I was so damned pleased with your solution to the situation."

"My solution? What did I do?"

"Why, son, it's still hard for me to realize that you don't remember anything about it. You married her."

Chapter Three

Tim drove toward the Barringer homestead on auto-pilot, still in shock from Charlie's revelation. He was married? He couldn't seem to grasp all the implications.

Unfortunately, the more Charlie had revealed to Tim about his forgotten past, the more questions arose. Yet Tim knew he couldn't stay any longer. Elisabeth had been right to insist that Charlie rest. He didn't need to get excited.

As far as that was concerned, Tim hadn't needed it, either. His head pounded as though a fife and drum corps had taken over space inside his skull for interminable practice.

Elisabeth . . . my wife, he thought, tentatively returning to the subject of the shock he'd received. His mind kept returning to the idea much like a tongue returns to the site of a lost tooth . . . probing for pain or for sensation of some kind. At the moment all he could feel was bewilderment.

What the hell was he doing married? If Charlie was to be believed, it had been Tim's idea to marry. But then, could Charlie be believed? He was a devious old coot, as sly as they come. But Tim could think of no reason he would agree to such an arrangement, even if it had been Charlie's idea.

And what about Elisabeth? What were her thoughts on the subject? She could have told him this morning . . . could have explained. As a matter of fact, as soon as he got to Charlie's place he'd demand some—

Charlie's place: that sprawling countryside that was measured in miles rather than acres, that was already listed in many of the historical guidebooks of the area. Charlie's place until he died, whereupon it would become Elisabeth's property. Elisabeth, his wife.

What the hell had he gotten himself into? He was no rancher—or miner, either, come to that. Although he had his little ski cabin in southwest Colorado and a condo in Denver, Tim didn't consider himself a person with much in the way of property that needed managing. He was gone too much of the time. It was no accident that there was no one in his life who had any claims on him or his time. Greg and Brandi were the closest people to him, and they had learned years ago not to expect to hear from him regularly.

Greg and Brandi. What would they think of his sudden marriage? He could almost hear Greg laughing now. Brandi would probably be wanting to share recipes and baby clothes with Elisabeth.

His foot slipped off the accelerator at the sudden thought of baby clothes. He hadn't thought to ask Charlie how long he'd been married, but it couldn't have been more than a few weeks. Could it be possible that he might already be—

No. What was he thinking of? The marriage had to be a farce, something he and Elisabeth had agreed to do for Charlie's sake. Tim knew himself well enough to know that he would never—

Damn it! What a hell of a time to get a knock on his head and a memory lapse. Here he was in a personal crisis, not to mention the precarious state of Charlie's health. What a ridiculous time to lose track of a few rather vital weeks in his life.

By the time he turned in at the gate of the Barringer place, Tim was tired, hungry, in pain and more than a little angry that his mysterious dearly beloved had omitted to tell him a few basic facts earlier in the day.

She could have at least explained why they were sharing a bed. It might have eased his conscience somewhat when he'd had to face Charlie.

He followed the winding black-top road through the hills until the lights from the hulking mansion came into view. It was certainly ostentatious enough, Tim had to admit. He also knew that to Charlie, who had been born there, it was home. Perhaps Elisabeth felt the same way.

If that was the case, why would her brothers not want her to keep it? There were so many undercurrents in the situation, the nuances of which were still uncertain to him. He needed more information.

"Hang tough, Charlie," he said out loud. "Don't let us down now. We both need you."

He pulled into the parking space he generally used whenever he was visiting, near the multicar garage. As he got out of the car Tim could hear Charlie's dogs barking from their pen. Living this far out in the country might bother Elisabeth, now that she was alone.

But she isn't alone, he had to remind himself, walking up the steps to the front door. *She has you.* Why didn't he find the thought more comforting?

He no sooner closed the front door behind him than the foyer seemed to fill with people. Or maybe because of his head, everyone seemed to have a double. Mrs. Brodie appeared from the kitchen, and Elisabeth came down the stairway.

His eyes were drawn to the cool blond freshness of the woman who slowly descended to where he stood watching her. She had changed into a matching sweater and skirt of pale green. Her hair, still braided, was in a coil at the nape of her neck. He wondered if she had any idea how the hairstyle accentuated the purity of her facial bone structure.

Tim had never seen a picture of her father, Charlie's son, but if Elisabeth was any indication, he'd been a striking man.

"Oh, Mr. Walker, I'm so glad you're home. I was beginning to worry about you, what with your head and all. I was afraid this was too soon for you to be out of bed. What if you'd passed out or something trying to drive home? Elisabeth couldn't have taken too much more happening to her at the moment, I'm afraid.''

Although he heard Mrs. Brodie, Tim couldn't seem to bring his gaze away from Elisabeth as she paused on the bottom step, her eyes even with his.

''Were you worried?'' he asked her in a low voice as though no one else was around.

Her eyes flickered to Mrs. Brodie hovering in the background, then she met his gaze. ''I was a little concerned. You said you didn't plan to stay long with Granddad.''

He took her hand, feeling the slender coolness of her fingers. ''That was my intention. However, he was so full of rather astounding information, I'm afraid I lost track of the time.'' He watched a faint wash of rosy color fill her cheeks.

''Are you ready to eat, Mr. Walker? Elisabeth suggested we wait for you.''

He turned and smiled at the woman standing nearby. ''Yes, Mrs. Brodie. I'll just run upstairs and wash up.'' Still holding Elisabeth's hand, he squeezed it slightly and said, ''Thank you for waiting for me.'' Feeling a strange reluctance to lose contact with her, Tim dropped Elisabeth's hand and stepped past her to go upstairs.

He had almost reached the top of the stairs when her voice stopped him.

''Tim?''

He turned and found her standing at the bottom of the stairway alone.

''Yes?''

"Did Granddad say... Did the two of you talk about—What I mean is—"

"We'll discuss it later, Elisabeth. I still have many questions. I hope you'll help me with some of the answers."

She nodded, looking almost unsure of herself for a moment. From everything he had learned about her today, it was no doubt a rare moment, and as such, should be savored.

They ate at a small table set into the alcove of the large dining area. As many times as Tim had visited Charlie he still hadn't gotten used to the sense of stepping back in time whenever he was there.

Since Mrs. Brodie continued to check on them periodically, Tim had no desire to start an intimate discussion with Elisabeth over dinner. Therefore he kept the conversation casual.

"I was surprised to find such an up-to-date medical facility in a town as small as Cripple Creek," he commented after a particularly long silence had stretched between them.

Elisabeth smiled. "Yes. Well, that's because Granddad donated most of the money for it. As a matter of fact, that was one of the arguments he used to convince me he'd be better off staying there than at home. Since he'd put so much money into it, he deserved to be their star patient."

Tim laughed. "That sounds just like him."

Elisabeth smiled her agreement, her eyes filled with sadness. "I don't want to lose him."

"I can understand that. He's really something."

"How long have you know him?"

"I'm not sure. Ten years, maybe. We met in Washington."

"He thinks a great deal of you."

Tim picked up his cup and sipped the steaming coffee before he answered her in a deliberate tone. "He must, to have allowed his adored granddaughter to marry me."

Elisabeth glanced toward the kitchen door before looking at him. "I suppose," was all she replied.

After they finished their meal, Elisabeth suggested they cross the hall to what at one time would have been called the parlor. A cheerful fire danced in the fireplace, giving the large room a cozy appearance.

"How's your head feeling?" Elisabeth asked after they sat in matching chairs across from each other.

"Better."

"Did you take the medication prescribed for you while you were upstairs?"

"No. I've switched to aspirin. Even though it doesn't take the pain away, it manages to dull it somewhat without knocking me out. We need to talk."

She glanced at her hands clasped in her lap but did not respond.

"Why didn't you tell me this morning that we were married?"

Elisabeth raised her head and looked at him, obviously surprised at the line of questioning. For reasons he didn't quite understand, Tim discovered their marriage was at the top of his list of needed answers.

"I wasn't deliberately hiding the information, you know. I just wasn't sure how to explain . . . how much you remembered about everything."

"It didn't occur to you that I might have been more than a little unnerved to discover that I was sleeping with Charles Barringer's granddaughter? With no memory of a ceremony I drew an erroneous, although perfectly natural, conclusion that was more than a little disconcerting."

She grinned, and he was surprised to see the mischievous light that appeared in her eyes. "Were you afraid that if Granddad knew about it, he would get out his shotgun?" she teased lightly.

"Knowing Charlie the way I do, I was more than a little afraid he'd use the shotgun on me rather than listen to any explanation I might offer. Given the fact that I couldn't remember a thing, I couldn't even come up with an explanation."

"You poor dear."

"Yes. You can understand my concern."

"Without a doubt. Granddad's temper is legendary."

"You don't seem to find it troublesome, though."

Her smile seemed to recall certain memories that Tim suddenly wished he shared. "Well, I've had considerable practice dealing with his temper."

"So he said. He's rather impressed with your temper, from what I gathered."

Her smile grew. "Nonsense. He just enjoys maligning my character, which doesn't surprise me in the least."

"Are the doctors giving him much more time?"

She shook her head. "They don't understand how he's hung on this long. They've given up cautioning him about his routine. He thrives on visitors, enjoys berating the nurses and gives the doctors fits. Yet all the tests show that his heart is worn out. He could go any time."

"He suggested that we marry, didn't he?"

Her gaze searched his face as though looking for something. He didn't know what it was. When she spoke her voice was lightly casual. "He's always worried about me and my welfare. It's a habit that he can't seem to break."

"What I don't understand is why you were willing to go through such a thing just to appease him."

"Don't you?" Her gaze wandered to the fire and she studied it for several moments in silence. "I would probably do anything I could to help him rest more and worry less."

That made sense to him. A lot of sense. Charlie might see her as an independent, modern female. Perhaps she was, in many ways. But her love had willingly placed her in emotional chains. The question was, for how long?

"I'd appreciate it if you would fill me in on our agreement."

Her green-eyed gaze turned slowly to meet his once more. "Our agreement about what?"

"The marriage. I'm sure I explained to you that with my work and general life-style, marriage doesn't really fit in to my plans." When she didn't comment, he went on. "I can understand that neither one of us wanted him upset. Now he can go, knowing that I'll be here for you." He thought about that for a moment. "And I intend to be, don't get me wrong. I know it isn't going to be easy for you to get through the next few months. He filled me in on Jason's and Marcus's probable reaction. You won't have to face them alone."

Her tone was level when she said, "I'm not afraid of Jason or Marcus."

"Well, that's good. Then you won't mind my admitting that although I'm not actually afraid of them, I'm not looking forward to making their acquaintance."

"Don't worry. I'll protect you, if need be."

She had spoken so quietly that for a moment he didn't believe he'd heard her correctly. She hadn't changed expression as she made her outrageous comment.

Tim couldn't help it. He began to laugh. Dear God, but she was adorable. This was the woman Charlie had thought needed protection? He almost felt sorry for her brothers. Almost, but not quite. She watched him, a slight smile appearing on her face.

"Thank you," he managed to say after a moment. "You don't know how much that relieves my mind. I know I'll be able to sleep better at night."

She chuckled but did not reply.

"Speaking of sleeping. I'm surprised that we're sharing a bedroom, under the circumstances. Since Charlie isn't here he wouldn't need to know our sleeping arrangements."

"He'd find out."

"From Mrs. Brodie, I suppose."

She shrugged. "Who knows how Granddad learns about things? For all I know he has this whole house wired for sound."

"That's a thought."

"Would you prefer the privacy of your own bedroom?" she asked.

"Not necessarily," Tim drawled. "I rather enjoyed waking up to find Sleeping Beauty in my bed this morning."

He was delighted to see that his remark caused her color to heighten. She wasn't nearly so bold nor so brave as she would like him to think.

"Can you give me some of the details of our marriage?"

She made a slight movement, almost as though she had flinched, but since her gaze remained calm and perfectly steady, Tim decided he must have imagined a reaction.

"What sort of details?"

"Oh, the usual. When . . . where . . . who was there. You know the sort of thing."

"We were married May second in a private ceremony in Granddad's room at the hospital. Because of the suddenness of the decision, two of the nurses witnessed it. The judge who married us is a long-time friend of Granddad's."

Tim found all this very disorienting. He also realized, with something like dismay, that he had no idea what day it was.

He rubbed his forehead, frowning.

"You're in pain, aren't you?" Her voice sounded soft and concerned.

"I'm more confused than anything. What's today's date?"

"It's Friday, May twentieth."

He'd been married for almost three weeks and had no memory of it. None whatsoever. He leaned his head against the back of the chair and closed his eyes.

"Why don't you get some rest, Tim? You've done too much today, you know."

He opened his eyes and met her gaze. Ignoring her comment, he asked, "Who found me?"

"Found you? What do you mean?"

"When I got my concussion."

"Oh! One of the ranch hands and I. We'd taken the dogs with us."

"Would you be able to find the spot again?"

She thought about that for a moment. "I suppose. If you think it's necessary. Sam guessed that your horse may have been spooked when you weren't prepared for it, and that you were thrown off."

"Sam's the ranch hand?"

"Actually, he's the foreman, I suppose."

"I don't know him?" That was a safe bet if Sam thought Tim could fall off his horse.

"No."

"Do your brothers know we're married?"

Elisabeth started to answer, then stopped for a moment as though puzzled. "You know, I'm not sure. They haven't heard it from me, but I don't know if Granddad told them or not."

"Do they know he's in the hospital?"

"Yes. I called them."

"Have they been to see him?"

She nodded. "Jason flew out in his company's jet after Granddad's heart attack. Marcus was unavailable at the time, but I think he's called and talked with him."

"What do your brothers do?"

She grinned. "I've never known anyone with so many questions. I almost feel as though I'm on the witness stand. You leap from one subject to another without warning."

If she could only understand how he felt. For every question he verbalized, five more popped up in his head. It was as though he had walked into the middle of a movie with no idea of the plot or who the characters were. Worse than that, he felt as though he was supposed to be a part of the story and had no clue as to what his lines were.

When he didn't respond, she sighed. "Tim, please go to bed. I promise to answer more questions tomorrow. But you really need to rest."

"Will you come tuck me in and tell me a bedtime story?" He couldn't resist teasing her.

"Was that part of our agreement?"

"How the hell should I know? Our agreement, as you call it, could have been anything." He knew he sounded irritable, but it wasn't half what he was feeling at the moment.

She eyed him for a moment in silence, then got up. "All right. Here's what I'll do. Why don't you take a nice, hot shower and try to relax your neck and shoulder muscles a little. Afterward I'll give you a massage. That should help you sleep."

Slowly Tim came to his feet. "Why would you do that?"

She shrugged. "It wouldn't be the first time."

"You mean since my concussion."

Her color heightened slightly. "No. Before."

"You're in the habit of giving me massages?"

"I wouldn't call it a habit."

Why was she being evasive? Though he tried, Tim could not read anything in her expression.

What sort of relationship had evolved between the two of them during the two weeks after their wedding and before his injury? From the evidence it would seem that they shared the same room and bed.

Tim had trouble with that one. Perhaps he would agree to a sham marriage if he felt strongly enough about the reasons for it, but would he needlessly torture himself by spending night after night next to this warm, attractive, intelligent woman?

He felt that he knew himself fairly well and yet that appeared to be wholly out of character for him. Chivalrous? Perhaps. Martyr material? Not likely.

So what was the answer? He wasn't even sure of the question. And if he could formulate it, to whom would it be directed? Elisabeth didn't know him well. How could she possibly explain his motivation?

Elisabeth walked over to him and companionably linked her arm with his. "Come on. I'll walk you upstairs."

He had a hunch that she had used that particular form of cajoling with her grandfather with almost certain positive results. However, he wasn't her grandfather and his reaction to her soft breast pressing lightly against his forearm was anything but familial.

If he didn't know better, Tim decided, he'd swear he'd been out of his mind for much longer than a few days. How else could he explain his recent actions? Or perhaps the knock he'd gotten on his head wasn't the true cause of the amnesia. Blanking out his memories was probably the only way he knew to survive their current sleeping arrangements without a complete loss of sanity.

Now he was going to begin more memories. Tim had always considered himself to be a survivor.

Would he be able to survive his celibate role under these conditions?

Only time would tell.

Chapter Four

The sound of a phone ringing late at night was ominous to Tim, probably because good news never seemed to travel in such a manner. Only the urgency of bad news gave impetus to the need to arouse others from their sleep.

Elisabeth answered the phone on the first ring, turning on the lamp beside her. Tim raised himself on his elbow, running his other hand through his hair, while he tried to understand the message she was being given.

He already knew.

She had her back to him and was giving monosyllable replies as she continued to listen. The soft light highlighted the long waves of hair that fell across her shoulders and along her back.

He didn't remember her getting into bed with him. The last he recalled was the quiet strength of her warm hands kneading the muscles in his back and shoulders, relaxing him, soothing him, easing the pain that seemed to slowly recede in his head.

Tim glanced at his watch. It was almost four o'clock . . . the darkest hour . . . just before dawn.

Elisabeth murmured something, then carefully replaced the receiver, turned out the light and rolled onto her back, staring into the darkness.

"Charlie?" Tim felt a need to get her to talk to him.

"Yes."

"Who called?"

"Neil Swanson, Granddad's attorney." Her voice showed no emotion whatsoever. "Granddad had left strict instructions at the hospital. Whenever he went, he wanted Neil to be the first one notified. Neil knew what Granddad wanted done."

"Which is?"

She sighed. "He didn't want me having to call and tell anyone or having to worry about the details. Neil said he'd call back later and let me know the time set for the services." She sounded empty somehow.

"He was trying to take some of the burden off you."

"Yes."

They lay there in the dark, together and yet apart. Because of the size of the bed there was no reason for them to touch, and Tim hesitated to encroach on her space, but he had such a fierce need to comfort her, if only she would allow it.

Slowly he moved his hand until it brushed against her arm. He gave her the opportunity to withdraw, and when she didn't he took her hand, threading his fingers between hers.

"I'll never forget the first time I saw him," she said several minutes later. "My mother had died the week before. She'd been the ranch cook as far back as I could remember, and now that she was gone, the owner wasn't really sure what to do with me."

"Where were you living?"

"In Arizona. When my dad was alive they lived in Tucson. After his death she needed to find a place where she could look after me as well as work. Since she'd been raised on a ranch, it was what she knew best."

"Then Charlie showed up."

He could almost hear the smile in her voice. "Yes. Such a big man, with a booming voice and a no-nonsense manner. He was at the ranch house one afternoon when I got in from school. Said he'd just gotten word about my mother. Said he was my grandfather."

When she didn't say anything more Tim prodded her, knowing it would help her if she talked. "Were you surprised?"

"I told him I didn't know what he was talking about. My grandfather had been dead for years. That's when he said he was my dad's father, and nobody had ever accused him of being dead. Nobody had better try." Her voice caught at the words, and he knew she was trying to choke back a sob.

Tim moved toward her and pulled her into his arms. She gave no resistance, allowing herself to be turned like a limp rag doll.

"You know, I've known for some time that he was going." Her words were beginning to blur with the sound of tears. He tucked her face into his shoulder and began to stroke her back, molding her to his broad frame. "Losing my mom was such a shock because it was so sudden, with no warning. She woke up one morning not feeling well, and by night she was gone. I thought that was why it hit me so hard. Losing her was so unexpected. She was all I had."

She sniffed, and Tim rolled them both so that he could reach for a tissue from a box beside the bed. She lay partly sprawled across him, without awareness of the intimacy they shared.

He handed her the tissue.

"It doesn't really help, though, knowing you're going to lose them. No matter how prepared you are, you're never ready." The tears were coming fast.

Tim didn't say anything. He reached for more tissue and continued to hold her to him, lightly pressing her to him to remind her that she wasn't alone.

"Dear God. I loved him so much." The dam broke, and her sobs shook her. Her arms came around his neck, and she clutched him convulsively to her.

For the first time since he'd awakened the day before Tim recognized how important it was that he was there. She needed him, and somehow he had known that. Perhaps she maintained a show of pride and strength to the world around her—she was Charles Winston Barringer's granddaughter, after all—but at the moment she needed Tim, and he was thankful that he was there for her.

When the first storm of grief had passed somewhat, Tim stroked her hair away from her flushed face and said, "He loved you more than he ever loved anyone."

She caught her breath. "Did he say that?"

"Those were his exact words."

"But I was always arguing with him."

"What do you think kept him in such fine form? He thrived on arguments. You know that."

Her watery chuckle reassured him.

"He wanted you to be happy. I know he didn't want you to grieve over him."

"I heard that often enough!"

"He was tired, love. He was ready to go home."

"I know. I know it's selfish of me to wish for more. But he's all I have."

"You have me." Tim didn't know where the words came from, he only knew, when he heard them, that they were right. She had him for as long as she wanted him. She was important to him, her happiness was important to him. He never wanted her to feel that she was alone again.

He could feel her body stiffening and knew that she had just then become aware of how closely he held her to him. Despite the seriousness of the situation his body had readily responded to her. He had no control over his physical reaction to her. He could only hope that she knew he would not act upon it.

When she tried to pull away from him, he immediately loosened his hold on her. She scooted away. He didn't move but continued to lie on his back.

"I'm sorry. I didn't mean to try to drown you."

"That's just one of the functions of a husband, didn't you know?"

"You don't even remember being a husband."

Her voice sounded discouraged, almost defeated.

"Maybe not, but give me time. I'll get the hang of it."

"I doubt that you'll be around long enough."

He couldn't read anything into her comment and now that she was no longer within touching distance, he couldn't tell by touch whether she was relaxed or tense.

"Why should I leave?"

"Why should you stay? Charlie's gone now. He died happy, knowing I was being looked after."

"Maybe I like looking after you. I might want the job on a permanent basis."

He felt the bed move and knew that she had shifted. Her voice sounded closer. "Just a few hours ago you were enumerating all the reasons you weren't the marrying kind."

Damn. She was a hard woman to argue with. She could use his own words against him. "That was because I was still shocked to find out that I was married."

"I see. Now you're used to the idea."

He moved his hand until he brushed against her, then rubbed his palm against her cheek. "Let's just say that the idea has more and more appeal to me."

He heard her breath catch in the silence of the room.

"It would be different if you could remember," she finally said.

"Remember what?"

"Oh, nothing in particular, I suppose. I have such a sense of taking advantage of you. I could tell you anything and you would have to accept it."

"Is that what you're doing?"

"No! I wouldn't take advantage of you or the situation in that way."

"I never believed you would."

He moved his hand so he could feel the pulse in her neck, its rapid beat registering her agitation.

"Will you let me hold you? I promise not to take advantage of you, either. I just want you to know I'm here for you."

Almost childlike, Elisabeth returned to his arms, placing her head on his shoulder, resting her hand on his chest.

"Do you think you can get some rest?" he asked after a moment. "I have a hunch we're both going to need it today." She felt so good in his arms . . . as though she was where she belonged.

"I suppose. I need to start planning when I'm going to leave." She sounded drowsy, as though she were slowly drifting toward sleep.

"Leave? Leave where?"

"Leave here. I'm sure that Jason and Marcus will push to get me out of here as soon as possible."

"You think Charlie will leave this place to them?" He kept his voice carefully neutral.

"Of course. It's been in their family for a hundred years. It's their birthright."

"It's yours, too."

"No, not really. Except for the past couple of years, I've only spent summers and school holidays here."

"How much time have Jason and Marcus spent here?"

She sighed. "It doesn't matter. It belongs to them."

"Did Charlie know how you felt about the place?"

"Of course. We talked about it years ago. He was in one of his patriarch moods, determined to arrange everyone's lives to suit him. He said he wanted me to have this place, and I told him it wasn't worth fighting over."

"What did he say?"

"Say? That's too polite a word. He roared. Whenever he couldn't get his own way, Granddad roared."

She shifted, her hand idly playing in the curls on his chest. "I finally convinced him I'd be fine. I've never needed his money...well, maybe right at first. What I needed was his love and attention, and he was lavish with that."

"Well—" Tim turned slightly so she was tucked firmly against his body "—it doesn't matter to me where we live. I've got a condo in Denver. Or we could buy a place wherever you want."

She raised her head, and he knew she was trying to read his expression in the dark. "Tim, I thought we were agreed that the reason for our marriage no longer exists. I appreciate your being here for me. Granddad was right about that. But I'm a big girl now. I can look after myself. I don't need a keeper, despite what you two think.''

Tim thoroughly appreciated the feel of her body so warm against his. He closed his eyes. He was beginning to see what Charlie had been warning him about. Elisabeth had a great deal of pride and more than her share of independence. He was definitely going to need his rest at the moment because when she found out that Charlie had disregarded her wishes about the homestead, Tim had a hunch he was going to bear the brunt of her reaction.

''Let's get some sleep,'' he murmured, patting her shoulder then letting his hand slide along her ribs to her waist.

Strange how much he was looking forward to the coming skirmish. She was a worthy opponent. Charlie had raised her well.

Tim coaxed Elisabeth into going for a horseback ride that afternoon, hoping to get her out of the house for a while.

Tim had learned from Mrs. Brodie that Elisabeth had been spending all her days at the hospital. No wonder she looked so fragile.

He wondered if that was what they had quarreled about the day he'd gone riding alone.

Tim had awakened and realized he was beginning to have flashbacks. The relief that swept over him was tremendous. The ache in his head seemed to have almost completely dissipated, returning only when he was tired or under unusual strain.

Some of the flashes he got were in the form of silent movies. He couldn't remember what they were saying to each other, but he recalled Elisabeth's flushed face and vehement attitude. He remembered walking away from her, going outside, and later he'd gone to the barn, which was located, along with several other outbuildings, almost a mile from the house.

Charlie had warned him she was stubborn. Well, so was he.

This time, however, she had agreed to go riding. The day had turned out warm, but a fresh breeze kept it from being uncomfortable.

Elisabeth's mount was a palomino gelding, his mane and tail the same color as her silver-blond hair. They made a striking pair. The green cotton shirt she wore reflected the green of her eyes as she seemed to drink in the view of the mountains that surrounded them.

"There's no place anywhere on earth quite as beautiful, is there?" she finally said after they had ridden in silence for a time.

"I have to agree."

"Have you always lived in Colorado?" she asked as they allowed their horses to follow an almost indiscernible trail.

"Except for when I was in the military."

"What do you do now?"

He glanced at her from the corner of his eye. Was she testing him for some reason? "Why do you ask?"

"Because you've never said. When I asked Granddad he muttered something about government work."

"That's about it."

"But that could be anything from mail carrier to senator and all sorts in between."

"I'm a troubleshooter. I check out a situation, then return and report my findings and conclusions."

"Like an auditor?"

He grinned. "Something like that."

"You must work for the IRS."

He laughed. "Why do you say that?"

"Well, you keep hedging. I would imagine that most people would react negatively to the idea of having an IRS agent in their midst."

"Only if they have something to hide."

"Doesn't everyone?"

Tim stood up in the saddle, taking the weight off his rear end for a moment, knowing that he was out of shape for riding for any length of time.

"What do you have to hide?" he asked, watching her profile.

Elisabeth quickly turned her head toward him. "Why, nothing. What makes you ask?"

"Because you never talk about your profession."

"My profession!"

"Charlie told me you're a writer."

She glanced away from him, scanning the horizon. "Granddad always exaggerated everything."

"He said you sold a book once."

"Why would he tell you about that?"

"He was explaining how you wouldn't even let him pay for your education. Instead, you insisted on paying him back out of the money you received for a book."

Without looking at him, she said, "No wonder you were so long returning yesterday. He must have told you my life story."

"I was interested. Remember, as far as I was concerned I met you for the first time yesterday."

She was quiet, and Tim allowed the silence to spread between them. After a while Elisabeth spoke again, her voice musing. "I've always been interested in American history, particularly the Western United States. I enjoy reading about it, finding out little-known facts, then weaving stories about the people that lived in that time."

"Was that why you were willing to move to Colorado?"

She shook her head. "I moved back because Granddad needed me. He was too proud to admit it, but we both knew it. He was getting too old to travel. It really didn't matter where I lived. So I came home."

Tim glanced at the sun. "We'd better head back, don't you think?"

Elisabeth looked at her watch. "I didn't mean to stay out so long. Mrs. Brodie has so much to do, getting ready for everyone. And the phone was ringing off the wall."

"Why do you think I got you out of there? I suggested she call someone in to help her with the cooking and cleaning."

"I should have thought of that."

Tim tightened his hold on the reins, watching as she did the same thing. They turned and started back.

"How well do you know Jason and Marcus?"

"I've only seen them a couple of times. They attended one of Granddad's social gatherings in Washington when I met them for the first time."

"What do you think of them?"

Her voice went flat. "I have no opinion of them one way or the other."

"What do they think of you?"

She shrugged. "I'm sure you'll be able to ask them. According to Neil, they told him they'd fly in some time today."

"They'll stay at the homestead?"

She looked surprised. "Of course. It belongs to them now. Where else would they stay?"

Thanks a lot, Charlie, Tim thought.

Tim and Elisabeth entered the house through the kitchen. Two young women were working there, and the savory scents coming from the stove and oven promised ample nourishment to everyone. The women glanced up with shy smiles but quickly resumed what they were doing.

Mrs. Brodie came through the door from the hallway just as Tim and Elisabeth reached it.

"Oh! There you are. Jason and Marcus Barringer arrived a few minutes ago. They're having coffee in the library."

Elisabeth glanced down at her casual attire and made a face.

"Why don't you go upstairs and change? I'll go speak with them."

She was unable to mask her relief before she replied, "It doesn't matter. I'll have to see them sometime."

"They can wait a little longer. And you'll be more comfortable."

"That's true. If you're sure..."

Tim couldn't resist leaning over and placing a soft kiss on her mouth. Her lips tasted and felt as enticing as they looked. "I'm sure." *About a lot of things,* he added to himself.

Fully aware that he smelled of horses and outdoors, he crossed the foyer to the library and opened the door. As he entered the room, two men came to their feet and faced him.

They were obviously brothers—both tall, blond and tanned, both wearing dark business suits with vests and ties, both sizing him up as he was them. These men were nobody's fools. Elisabeth wasn't the only one who had inherited intelligence and charm.

The one on the left stepped forward with a dignified smile. Holding out his hand, he said, "I don't believe we've met. I'm Jason Winslow Barringer, and this my brother, Marcus Chandler Barringer. You must be the old man's foreman. I want you to know that you need have no concern about your position here. Our reports show that you have been doing a fine job managing the place." He glanced at his brother, who added a solemn nod of approbation.

Tim took Jason's hand and shook it firmly, then shook hands with Marcus. They were good. He had to give them that. The look, the tone of voice, the just-right grip of the hand. It was all there in the most subtle way imaginable, carefully putting him in his niche in their life.

He smiled. "I'm sure Sam's going to be immensely pleased to hear you approve of his efforts, gentlemen."

"Sam?"

"Charlie's foreman. As for me, well, I'm just part of the family... your brother-in-law, Tim Walker."

Neither man showed any reaction to his announcement other than to exchange a charged glance.

"Elisabeth's husband," he added helpfully.

"Ah. Elisabeth," Jason said smoothly. "Yes. The attorney mentioned that she was still here."

"Still?" Tim repeated softly.

"What my brother means to say," Marcus interjected, "is we weren't sure until we asked if she intended to remain here until after the funeral."

"Where did you think she would go?"

Once again the men exchanged a look.

"This is the first we knew that she had married," Jason offered.

"Yes, I got the impression that the three of you aren't particularly close."

Marcus coughed, and received a dirty look from his brother. He gave Tim a deprecating smile. "I know Charlie seemed to enjoy perpetuating the myth that Elisabeth was dad's daughter. We saw no reason to dispute the matter. She kept him entertained these last few years. That was the important thing."

"I see. Then you don't consider her your sister?"

Jason's chuckle was well-bred. "Definitely not, although I never ruled out the possibility that she was

actually Charlie's bastard daughter. There is a certain
family resemblance. I wouldn't put it past Charlie to
cover his own peccadilloes with a story that makes him
look like a benevolent patriarch rather than a scan-
dalous old goat.''

"So what you are saying is that Elisabeth could very
well be your aunt?" Tim walked over to the empty
fireplace and leaned against the mantle, his arms
crossed.

"What difference does it make?" Marcus asked,
clearly irritated with the whole subject. "The old
man's gone now. I'm sure he's been generous enough
with her. No doubt he's made some provision for her
in the will. We have no argument with that."

Tim nodded. "Very generous of you both, I'm
sure."

There was a tap on the door, and Tim noticed that
it was Jason who responded, already taking over as
master of the household.

"Come in."

Mrs. Brodie stuck her head around the door.
"Would you gentlemen care for more coffee?"

Before either brother could respond, Tim smiled
and said, "Thank you, Mrs. Brodie. I'd appreciate
some fresh coffee about now."

Both men looked at him sharply, then returned to
the comfortable leather chairs that were grouped
around the fireplace.

"What do you do, Tim?" Jason inquired politely,
crossing his legs without disturbing the sharp crease in
his trousers.

"About what, Jason?"

"He's asking about your employment," Marcus prodded.

"Oh! Well, I'm what could be considered a private consultant."

"A consultant on what subject?"

"Oh, this and that."

Mrs. Brodie entered the room carrying a full tray. In a few strides Tim was by her side relieving her of her burden. She smiled her thanks, picked up the smaller tray and left the room.

Tim set the tray on the coffee table and sat on the sofa. He poured himself some coffee and leaned back, savoring the aroma as though he were alone in the room.

Marcus stood, walked to the table and poured two cups of coffee, giving one to Jason.

Jason took the cup and saucer and asked Tim. "Where's Elisabeth?"

"Upstairs changing. She wasn't aware we had company until we got back from riding." He took a sip of the coffee and gave a nod of approval. "Are you two married?"

Jason replied. "I am. Marcus is divorced. Why do you ask?"

Tim shrugged. "Just wondered. Great idea, marriage. Helps to keep your back warm at night, your belly full—" He smiled at the two men before he continued. "I'd say it manages to take care of all a man's needs."

"Is that what you'd say?" Jason repeated softly, barely veiling the contempt in his voice. "Just how long have you and Elisabeth been married?"

Tim shrugged. "Not long. It was love at first sight. Ya know what I mean? I took one look at her ... she took one look at me ... and there we were. We were married by the end of the week."

"Were you, indeed?" Jason murmured. "How interesting. What did Charlie think about that?"

"Don't know that I ever heard him say, now that you mention it. Of course he was in the hospital when we met."

"Of course."

"But Elisabeth doesn't have to worry about being alone now. She has me."

Marcus carefully placed his cup and saucer on the table beside his chair and came to his feet. He walked to one of the long, narrow windows and gazed outside. "Are you under the impression that Elisabeth is going to inherit this place?"

"It's her home, isn't it?" Tim asked.

Jason leaned forward, placing his elbows on his knees. "Not necessarily, no. She has been living here as a companion for Charlie. We saw no reason to disturb the arrangement. He needed someone. She was available."

"I understood that you two lived back East somewhere?"

"What does that have to do with anything?"

Tim shrugged. "I can't see any reason you'd want this place."

Jason nodded. "I'm sure you can't."

"I got the impression you both have more money than you'd ever be able to spend in several lifetimes."

A flash of distaste rippled across Jason's features. "There are other things in life besides money."

"Such as?"

"This place represents our heritage. I doubt that you would understand."

Tim finished his coffee and stood. Stretching his arms above his head, he said, "You're probably right." He glanced at Marcus, who still had his back to the room. "I've enjoyed chatting with you, gentlemen. Guess I'd better go upstairs and get cleaned up for dinner. Something smelled awfully good in the kitchen when I came through. I suppose you're staying for dinner?"

Jason seemed to have a little trouble moving the stiff muscles in his face into the semblance of a smile. "Naturally."

Tim nodded. "Then we can chat over dinner. Get better acquainted."

He closed the door quietly behind him and started up the stairway, wishing that Charlie was there. He would be enjoying all this immensely. Damn, he was going to miss the man. Thank God he'd found Elisabeth.

Chapter Five

Charles Winston Barringer's last services were held in Colorado Springs. The church was filled to overflowing with Charlie's friends and business associates.

A public figure for most of his life, he had drawn many people to him. He had an uncanny ability to recognize potential and encourage others in their use of it.

Tim recognized many faces from Washington. Legislators, Cabinet members and others not as well known gathered to pay their last respects.

Tim was proud of Elisabeth. She had handled the meeting with Jason and Marcus with quiet dignity the night before. Today, with equal decorum, she accepted the condolences of those who knew her grandfather. How could anyone not love this woman, Tim found himself thinking, then blinked. Where had that thought come from?

They were leaving the church after the service, preparing to go to the cemetery, when Tim felt a firm pressure on his arm in the crush of people moving toward the door.

"Why don't you answer any of your phone messages?"

He recognized the voice, just as he had recognized the face earlier. "I've been busy," he murmured without turning his head, his arm still around Elisabeth's waist.

"Yes, I can see that."

"Is it urgent?"

"Call when you can."

"When are you returning?"

"Immediately."

The crowd began to thin in front of them. "I'll call tonight." He never looked around, but continued to the waiting limousine.

As soon as they were settled inside, Elisabeth asked, "Who was that man?"

"My employer."

"He doesn't look like anyone's employer."

Tim smiled. "He would consider that remark a compliment."

"What did he want?"

Tim shook his head. "I'm afraid to guess. He may want me to go to work."

"Oh."

"Then again, he may want to congratulate me on marrying you."

Without looking at him, she took his hand, which had been resting on his thigh. "Granddad was right. You've been such a help. I don't know how I would have gotten through all this without you."

"You would have done just fine."

"I just wish—"

When she didn't go on he glanced at her, but she had turned her face away.

"What do you wish?"

"Nothing. I guess I'm still having trouble realizing that he's gone."

"Yes. I feel the same way."

She finally turned and looked at him. "I'm glad that you knew him so well. That you understood him. So few people really did."

"He was a very private man."

"So are you."

Tim frowned. "Why do you say that?"

"I don't know. You just seem different, depending on who is around. I don't think you are ever truly relaxed and just being yourself."

"And what do you consider being myself?"

"Warm...and teasing...like Granddad in many ways."

"I don't feel like your grandfather, Elisabeth."

She grinned. "That's not what I meant. He trusted you. That's very important to me." She looked at the passing countryside. "There aren't too many people Granddad trusted."

"With good reason."

"I know."

They were quiet the rest of the way to the cemetery.

Neil Swanson, the attorney, had suggested earlier in the day that he meet them at the homestead after the services to read the will. Marcus had made it clear they had no more time to waste, and had quickly agreed.

Tim had reason to be grateful that Charlie had prepared him for what was to come. The five of them assembled in the library, and Tim could see that Neil was not looking forward to what was coming. However, Tim was impressed with the way the attorney dealt with the matter.

"There are several minor bequests in Charlie's will that I won't go into at the moment, if you don't mind," Neil began. "Each of you will receive a copy of the will. The original has already been placed on file at the Teller County courthouse." He took his time looking at each of them. When his eyes met Tim's, Tim realized that Charlie must have told Neil that Tim knew what was coming.

Neil began to read Charlie's instructions regarding property in the East, stocks, bonds and other securities that were divided equally between Jason and Marcus. The amount was substantial. They took it as their due.

"I leave the remainder and residue of my estate, which shall include but not be limited to all cash on hand, CDs, automobiles and the real estate commonly known as the homestead located near Cripple Creek, Colorado and more particularly described in exhibit A attached hereto and made a part hereof, including all furniture and furnishings therein, to my granddaughter, Elisabeth Barringer, to be dealt with in whatever manner she shall choose and only at her sole discretion.''

The three Barringers appeared to be frozen in suspended animation. Tim and Neil exchanged a rueful glance.

''Why, that son of a—''

''I don't believe it! That old buzzard was crazy! He can't do that!''

Elisabeth was staring at Neil, her color nonexistent. Slowly she began to shake her head. ''I can't accept that—''

''Of course you can't!'' Jason agreed. ''That's preposterous! She has no right to any of this. She's just the bastard daughter of one of dad's or the old man's floozies. Who the hell does he think he is, anyway?''

''According to the documentation in my files, Charles Winston Barringer has sole and exclusive ownership of this property, and as the owner he can leave it to whomever he wishes.'' Without glancing up, Neil shuffled some papers before he continued. ''I also have here a copy of Elisabeth Barringer's birth certificate, which states her father's name as Charles Winston Barringer, Jr. In addition, I have copies in Spanish of the dissolution of marriage between Nancy Winslow Barringer and Charles Winston Barringer, Jr., and a certificate of marriage, also Spanish, between Catherine Ann Shelby and Charles Winston Barringer, Jr., dated eleven months prior to the birth certificate.''

Nice touch, Charlie. Tim made a mental salute to his friend. *You covered all the bases and dotted all the*

i's. Tim then winced at his use of the mixed meta-
phors.

Jason looked at Tim, his expression contemp-
tuous. "And you knew about all this, didn't you? You
moved right in on her, knowing that she was going to
get her hands on this place. No wonder you rushed her
into marriage." He got up and walked to the door,
Marcus following him. "Well, don't start spending
your money yet, you two. The man was senile. No
question about it. I'll see you both in court."

The room was very quiet after the two men left. Tim
watched Elisabeth closely, worried about her lack of
color. She seemed not to have heard Jason's threats.
When she finally spoke, she was looking at Neil.

"I don't want this place, Neil, or the money."

"Charlie wanted you to have it, Elisabeth."

"He knew how the others would react."

"Yes. He didn't care. He left me a letter to give to
you." Neil smiled. "You know Charlie. He knew you
would argue with him, but he had his reasons. At least
let him share them with you."

Tears trickled down her cheeks, but her voice rang
clear when she asked, "Where in the world did
Granddad manage to come up with fake divorce and
marriage papers?"

Neil looked startled, which reflected how Tim felt.
She knew?

"I'm not sure I understand what you're talking
about," Neil replied in a careful tone.

Elisabeth waved her hand as though brushing away
his protest. "My parents were never married. My father never divorced his first wife. I can't remember

how old I was when my mother explained all that to me. But they loved each other. That I know. That I truly believe. She kept all the letters he wrote to her whenever he had to be away from her. It didn't matter to either of them that another woman carried his name. My mother was in his heart. Her deepest grief was that he never had the chance to know about me and that I never had the chance to know him. His letters told me a great deal about him, though."

She looked at Tim. "My father was very much like his own father, ignored any of the rules that got in the way of what he wanted. If he had known about me I think he would have made other arrangements, but like Granddad, I think my father thought he was immortal."

"Charlie knew better," Tim pointed out.

"Yes," she admitted sadly. "I guess he did."

"He wanted to protect you as much as he could. These papers will encourage your brothers to leave you alone." Neil tapped the file in front of him.

"But what am I going to do with this place? It's too big for one person."

Neil smiled. "Don't forget your husband, Elisabeth. You may decide to have a large family. And it isn't as though you'll have a hardship keeping it running smoothly. The one thing you'll never have to worry about is running out of money."

Once again she made a brushing-away gesture. "The money doesn't matter."

"Charlie also said you would say that. He knew you very well." Neil stood, closing the file and placing it inside his briefcase. "Here is the letter he left for you.

Read it, think about it, then let me know if I can assist you in any way.''

He came around the desk and held out his hand to Tim, who came to his feet and took it. Charlie had assured Tim that Neil was a good lawyer. Tim was impressed with his character.

Tim walked with him to the door and made sure it was locked behind him. Night had fallen while they had been in the library. When he turned to rejoin Elisabeth he noticed Mrs. Brodie hovering near the stairway.

''Are you and Elisabeth going to be the only ones for dinner?''

''Yes, Mrs. Brodie.''

''I can serve any time.''

''Please do that. We'll be in shortly.''

Tim walked into the library. Elisabeth had not moved, nor had she made any effort to read the letter Neil had handed to her.

''This makes it more real, somehow,'' she murmured without looking at him. ''More real than the funeral service. He's really gone.''

''Yes.'' Tim took her hand and pulled her gently to her feet, then slid his arms around her, holding her close.

''He always gets his own way,'' she muttered distractedly, and he grinned while he soothed her with his touch.

''He would be pleased to know you think so.''

''He's probably watching all this right now, having the time of his life laughing.''

''I wouldn't be at all surprised.''

"What am I going to do?" She sounded so bewildered that his heart ached for her.

"Right now you're going to have dinner with your husband. Then I suggest a nice hot soaking bath, a soothing massage and a good night's sleep."

Her arms slipped around his waist, and she held him for a long moment. Then she tilted her head and looked at him. "I know I'm being weak, but I'm so glad you're here at the moment."

"I'll always be here for you, Elisabeth." Tim knew at that moment that he was stating a profound truth.

She shook her head. "No. You have your own life. I have mine. The play is over. The roles are done. But for tonight, I'm glad you're here."

He knew that she was in no condition for an argument. It didn't really matter. More and more of the past few weeks had been coming to him today. His memory was returning. There were still blank patches, but he felt certain they would come to him in time.

Charlie's explanation had managed to jog earlier memories. He knew now why Charlie had wanted him there; knew that the situation was going to get more serious; knew that Elisabeth needed him more than ever; and he felt grateful that Charlie had entrusted her welfare to him.

He also knew that it had not been Charlie's idea for Tim to marry Elisabeth. It had not been necessary.

What he couldn't remember was if Elisabeth knew the truth about Tim's reasons for marrying her. Charlie had known. If she knew, she had given him no indication of it.

They ate in companionable silence. He could feel her exhaustion almost as if it were his own. As soon as he got her to bed and asleep, he had some phone calls to make.

It was time to plan for the next stages. Too bad Charlie couldn't be there. He would have been in his element.

"You don't have to do this," Elisabeth murmured into her pillow, more than half asleep.

Tim decided that he must have a streak of masochism inside him, because he was actually enjoying the form of refined torture he had chosen for himself.

Elisabeth was lying in bed after her bath with no more than a light sheet draped enticingly across her delectable derriere. He sat beside her, rhythmically moving his hands from her shoulders down to the base of her spine...over and over...back and forth, his fingers sliding along the slight indentation of her spine. Her skin felt like warm satin, without a blemish, and Tim felt as though he were going to explode any minute with desire.

Slowly moving his hands up from her waist, he allowed his fingers to slide to either side of her ribs so they brushed the soft plumpness of her breasts. She shifted slightly, the movement causing the sheet to slide an inch or two lower, so her rounded hips were bared to his gaze to create further torment.

"I want to do it," he admitted, his voice sounding more than a little hoarse. This time when his hands made their routine trek downward he allowed them to glide over her hips, kneading them softly, then slide over her legs. This time his thumbs lightly skimmed the tender flesh of her inner thighs.

She quivered.

"You . . . must be . . . getting . . . tired . . ."

"I'm enjoying it, believe me."

Once again he began his upward journey, lightly caressing each curve and hollow, lingering at her breasts before moving on to her shoulders.

"I'm glad." She sighed.

He allowed his mind to drift in an effort to release some of the tension created by touching Elisabeth so intimately.

Charlie had been right. The first sight he'd had of Elisabeth almost brought him to his knees, he recalled with a smile.

As soon as he had received Charlie's cryptic note, he had placed a call to him. When Charlie told him what he needed, Tim wasted no time leaving Denver and driving directly to the hospital.

Charlie had needed his advice about the situation, and Tim had spent some time discussing the matter in detail before Elisabeth had arrived. Only later did Tim discover that Charlie had sent her off on some trumped-up shopping expedition in Colorado Springs so he would have the opportunity to see Tim in private.

When she walked through the hospital door that first day, Tim felt as though he'd caught a hard left hook square in his solar plexus.

She had glowed with health and vitality. Her eyes sparkled, and the smile she wore for her grandfather had been so filled with love it took Tim's breath away.

The sides of her hair had been caught up and pulled into a knot at the back of her head. The rest had hung in waves across her shoulders and down her back. Her dress was some floaty material that swirled around her knees, revealing shapely legs that he longed to touch.

She had paused in endearing confusion when she saw him, and Tim had managed to get to his feet. He could almost feel his mouth hanging open.

"I didn't mean to interrupt," she managed to say, feeling for the door handle without turning around.

"Nonsense!" Charlie winked at Tim. "You aren't interrupting a thing. Did you manage to buy out the stores today?"

She grinned. "The dress shops were safe, but I went wild in the office-supply stores. They were having a half-price sale on paper and disks for the computer and—" She laughed. "I can't resist a sale. You know that."

"Elisabeth, I want you to meet a friend of mine, Tim Walker. Tim lives in Denver. Happened to be passing through and called the house, found out I was in the hospital and decided to see what the hell I was doing here."

Tim held out his hand, wanting more than anything to be able to touch the woman standing there. "I'm very glad to meet you, Elisabeth."

She placed her hand in his. It felt so small and delicate, as though it could be easily crushed. Her green-eyed gaze met his with an almost stunned expression. Was it possible she was feeling the same strong attraction that had shaken him? Tim had never reacted this way before to anyone. He felt as though the very air around them shimmered with the energy that pulsed between them.

He had no idea how long they stood there, staring at each other. Her gaze seemed to flit over each of his features, noting the dark red hair, the blue eyes, the way his clothes fit his body, the message in his eyes. There was no way he could hide his reaction to her, so he didn't bother trying. He just stood there, absorbing her, suddenly aware that this woman might have the ability to exert more power over him than any other human being in the world.

"Well, I'm glad to see that you two seem to like each other," Charlie said with a chuckle. "Why don't you sit down and get acquainted."

Elisabeth seemed to realize for the first time that they had been standing staring at each other for some time, her hand still firmly clasped in Tim's. Her face flooded with fiery color.

"I've invited Tim to stay with us for a few days, if that's all right with you, Elisabeth."

His comment seemed to add to her confusion. "Of course, Granddad. You know it doesn't matter to me who you have at the house."

"It's a little different now, though, what with me laid up here. I'm afraid it will be up to you to keep him entertained."

Tim turned to protest, only to meet Charlie's wink, which Elisabeth failed to catch.

"Oh!" She still sounded flustered. "Well, there's not much to do unless you enjoy horseback riding, that sort of thing."

Tim grinned. "I have a hunch I'll be quite easy for you to entertain." He might as well have come out and told her how much he wanted to make love to her.

Charlie's chuckle sounded pleased.

Tim had followed her home from the hospital in his car that evening. After dinner they had sat in front of the fire and talked for hours, as though they were old friends trying to catch up on each other's news.

They had talked about the things they enjoyed doing, places they had visited, music they liked, books they'd read, but neither one had talked about their work or about Charlie's health.

She had accepted his visit as a casual one. He'd implied he was on a vacation of sorts, which he was. He'd told her about his cabin in the Rockies and how Greg and Brandi had met each other there.

Elisabeth had expressed a desire to meet them, and he had assured her that she would.

As the hour had grown later, the firelight had grown lower, their voices had softened and their conversation had lessened. They had sat on the sofa sharing glances. He had been so exhilarated to have found her. Until now, he hadn't known he had been searching.

Their kiss had been as inevitable as the dawn. His whole body had ached with the need to hold her. She had responded with a naturalness that sent desire spiraling through him.

By the time they finally paused for breath, they were both gasping. His chest shook with the force of his heart pounding, and he could see from the quivering of her breast that she had been affected in the same way.

Tim wondered if he was under some kind of spell. Had some magic dust been sprinkled on him when she walked into the room that made him forget everything in his life? His job? His responsibilities?

They were no longer important to him. Nothing was as important to him as Elisabeth.

He told Charlie the next day while Elisabeth had stepped out of the room.

"Yeah, I kinda noticed your reaction yesterday when you first saw her."

Tim shook his head, feeling dazed. "I know it sounds crazy. How can I possibly explain it when I don't understand myself what's happened?"

"The question I have is, and you'll have to excuse an old man's concern, but what do you intend to do about it?"

"Well, it's a little too soon to be talking about marriage, wouldn't you say?"

Charlie nodded. "Under normal circumstances, I'd have to agree with you. But then, these aren't normal circumstances."

Tim recalled the earlier conversation. How could he have forgotten all that Charlie had told him? He felt like a fool. She would be in danger just as soon as Charlie was gone. And Charlie knew he didn't have much time left. Tim nodded, seeing Charlie's point. "As her husband I would be in a much better position to protect her."

"Maybe. At least being her husband it would only be natural that you'd be hanging around the place all the time, sort of watching what's going on."

"Would she agree to it?"

Charlie's eyes sparkled. He nodded to the door as it was pushed open. "No time like the present to find out, is there?"

"Find out what, Granddad?" she asked, walking over to the other side of the bed from where Tim stood and taking Charlie's hand in both of hers.

"I guess I never told you about how impetuous my old friend Tim is. Being filled with integrity, he thought maybe he should talk with me first, that's all."

Her eyes sparkled as she looked across at Tim. Obviously she had gotten more sleep the night before than he had. When he'd finally forced himself to leave her at her bedroom door he'd spent the rest of the night imagining her in bed alone, imagining what it would be like if she weren't alone, and driving himself over the brink with his thoughts.

"I don't know, Granddad. Tim doesn't strike me as the impetuous type."

The strange thing about it was that she was right. Tim was anything but impetuous. He'd learned to make lightning decisions at times, to rely on his instincts, but he'd never applied that skill in his personal life.

He hadn't had a personal life.

Until now.

"I told Charlie I wanted to marry you," he said. drawling the words slightly, deliberately lingering on each one.

"Why?" she blurted out, then shook her head, embarrassed.

"The usual reasons, I guess. I have a sneaking hunch I'm not going to be able to get along without you in my life. The thing is, I don't particularly want to try. I was just discussing that when you walked in."

Charlie looked at Elisabeth. "You know my situation, darlin'. I haven't pulled any punches with you. Every day I'm here I consider a miracle. It would please me greatly to see you married to Tim before I'm gone."

"Granddad! You can't be serious! We just met."

Charlie nodded. "I know that. I'm the one who introduced you, don't you remember?" He shook his head. "I know it's unusual, and if you don't want to marry him, I don't want you to. What I want is for you to be happy. The thing is that I've known Tim for several years. You can't find yourself a better man, honey. You have no idea how unusual his reaction to you is. I've watched women around him before. He never notices them. He's told me time and time again that he didn't ever expect to marry anybody." He patted her hand. "He changed his mind as soon as he saw you. I think I knew it before he did."

Elisabeth's gaze found Tim's. "It's too soon."

Tim nodded. "Probably."

Charlie didn't say anything.

Elisabeth glanced at the man in the bed, then at Tim. "You really want me to marry him?" she whispered to her grandfather, her gaze caught up with Tim's.

"Only if that's what you want, honey."

She took a deep breath, then slowly released the air in her lungs. "All right."

As far as Tim could remember, Elisabeth had never said why she agreed to the marriage. Now as he watched her lying so relaxed on the bed beside him, asleep at last, he wished he could remember if they had discussed it later.

He recalled the simple ceremony, he recalled signing the marriage license and accepting the judge's congratulations, but he couldn't seem to bring into focus what had happened next.

There were still two weeks in his life that faded in and out. He remembered riding on the property, checking the area Charlie had told him about, the area Charlie was sure would draw others in their greed.

Charlie had been right. Like a novice, Tim had not protected his back. It wouldn't happen again.

His hands finally stopped moving across the silken expanse of his wife's uncovered body. More than ever he needed to understand his agreement with Elisabeth about the marriage. Had she insisted it would be a marriage in name only for the sake of her grandfather? She had certainly given him that impression since he'd been recovering from the blow to his head.

Were her explanations about their reason for sharing the same room and bed accurate? Would Charlie have cared, as long as they were legally wed? Tim thought not.

It was his wife's motives that he didn't understand, that he needed to know. Had he ever understood them? Ever known what they were?

He pulled the covers up, tucking them carefully around her. He needed to distance himself from her for a while or he would never sleep tonight. He could use the time to make some calls. Starting with one to Washington, to the man who didn't look as though he would be anybody's employer.

Chapter Six

The phone was answered on the first ring, despite the late hour.

"Hi, Max. It's me."

"You've created quite a stir, you know."

"How's that?"

"Don't give me that, Tim. Showing up at Charlie's funeral married to his granddaughter was bound to grab you some unneeded attention."

"It couldn't be helped."

"I understand your new in-laws are particularly curious about you."

Tim grinned. "They didn't waste much time. What have they found out?"

"Just what you knew they would. Despite all their strings, no one seems to have any information on you."

Tim began to laugh.

"Of course by now they're no doubt convinced you're operating under an alias."

"I'm sure they've also checked the legality of the marriage."

"So did I. When Charlie wants something done, he pulls in the big guns, doesn't he?"

"The judge happened to be available."

Max chuckled. "I'm going to really miss Charlie. He can never be replaced."

"True enough. Why were you looking for me?"

"Doesn't matter now. I had someone else handle it. What I need to know from you is what your status is now that you're married."

"I'm still working on that."

"Care to give me a few more details?"

Tim glanced around the library. He sat behind Charlie's massive desk, his feet propped up on the edge. The small desk lamp shed a pool of light on the green desk blotter. God, he was tired. He almost wished for the blessed oblivion of the pain pills.

"I'll try. You see, Charlie needed me to do some personal work for him. He knew what was going to happen when he died. There were a few matters he wanted taken care of, to make sure things went the way he wanted."

"Sounds like Charlie. The only man I know who would insist on his own way even from the grave."

"Yeah, well since it involved his granddaughter, I could see his point."

"Mmm."

That was one of the things he'd noticed, working with Max over the years. Max had the damnedest habit of making noncommittal sounds when he didn't want you to know what he was thinking.

"He knew that he was putting her in a certain amount of danger, but nothing I couldn't handle."

"So you sacrificed yourself on the altar of matrimony? Why, Tim, how altruistic of you."

"Go to hell."

He could hear Max's chuckle above the subtle hum of the long-distance line.

"So your work is now beginning."

"That's right."

"How long will it take?"

"From all indications, those he expects will give us some trouble will waste no time. The question is how they'll go about it. After meeting them I would hazard a guess that they won't play by any of the rules."

"Which is why Charlie called you in on it."

"Precisely."

"I take it we're discussing the Barringer brothers."

"What a sleuth you are."

"What do you intend to do?"

"No more than I have to. Neutralize them."

"They have no idea who you are, do they?"

"You've already gotten an accurate reading on them. They think I married Elisabeth to get my hands on this property. And they hate the fact that I'm already in possession. They aren't sure whether or not I know the true value of what we have."

"I take it you do, though."

"Charlie is very thorough in his briefing techniques."

Tim could almost hear Max thinking in the silence. Finally, Max muttered, "I just wish to hell he would have asked *me* if he could use you before pulling you in."

"You know as well as I do that you'd have agreed to it."

"Why didn't you let me know what you were up to?"

"Good question. As a matter of fact, I probably thought I had."

"What's that supposed to mean?"

"That I got a little careless a few days ago and got brained, which resulted in a little problem with my memory."

"What! Why didn't you let me know that sooner?"

"Why? So you could hold my hand? That's what my beautiful new wife is for."

"Are you saying you still haven't fully recovered?"

"Yeah, unfortunately. I think most of it's come back, but there's a few vague areas yet."

"Why haven't you asked for some help?"

Tim grinned. "My pride keeps getting in the way. But I've decided to call an old war buddy of mine to see if he'll play backup for me."

"Why don't I send someone?"

"I've already considered and rejected that idea. This is a delicate situation. I don't want Elisabeth any more upset than she is already. Losing Charlie has been rough on her. I figure if I have Greg come visit for a few days, she won't give it much thought."

"Gregory Duncan?"

"The same."

"Oh. Well, I couldn't find anyone better myself. I've always regretted the fact I couldn't recruit him."

"I don't know if he's available, but I intend to give him a call. I thought I might wait until things start heating up a little first so I can project a time frame."

"Isn't that a little risky, considering the tricks your mind's playing on you? If you thought you'd contacted me, there may be other things you thought you did but in fact have not done."

"I'm ninety percent certain I've remembered the important stuff. You just weren't that important in the overall scheme of things at the moment, boss."

"If you're hoping to get fired because of insults and insubordination, you're out of luck."

Tim laughed. "Well, would you consider an extended leave of absence, say for the next twenty to thirty years?"

Max paused before replying. "You're serious, aren't you?"

"It's something to consider. I don't like the idea of leaving Elisabeth for weeks at a time without contact."

"She wouldn't be without contact. You know we watch the families of our people when they aren't available. She would be safe."

"I meant direct contact between us. I'm ready to stay home, Max."

"There seems to be a rash of this sort of thing going around. I'm losing more good men this way."

Tim grinned. "You've gotten your pound of flesh over the years and you know it."

"I may use you on a consulting basis. I can't lose you altogether. You're too valuable."

"As a matter of fact, that's how I explained myself to my new brothers-in-law . . . as a consultant."

Max laughed. "One of these days that sense of humor of yours is going to get you in trouble."

"Well, all this girlish gossip is putting me to sleep, boss. Think I'll stumble upstairs to bed."

"Aren't you technically on your honeymoon these days?"

Don't I wish? "We've got time for all that later. First things first."

"My, I never suspected you of being the patient sort. Marriage has definitely changed you. You may end up downright civilized."

"Don't hold your breath. I'll check in when I need to. Otherwise you know how to get hold of me."

"Yes, but it doesn't do much good if you don't check your messages once in a while."

"I know. I'll do that right now."

"You can ignore mine. They're outdated."

"You're all heart."

"Sweet dreams, sweetheart."

Tim hung up, shaking his head. Then he retrieved the phone again and punched in the combination of numbers that hooked him into his answering machine. He listened, his smile growing as Max's early polite messages became more pointed and irascible, eventually coming close to abusive. He sobered, knowing that he'd made a bad slip not making sure Max knew where he was and why.

He could have been in trouble and needed help. Max's worried undertones had come across loud and clear. No doubt he'd been shocked to see Tim at the funeral.

It couldn't be helped.

Then he heard Brandi's voice.

"Hi, Tim. Since we haven't heard anything lately we assume you're out of the country on one of your hush-hush trips. In case you've forgotten, Cindy's got a birthday coming up in a few weeks—her first. Thought I'd give you a special invite to come help us celebrate. Anyway, give us a call when you get home. We'd love to see you. Greg sends his best."

There were several more calls on the machine, none of which were important enough to answer after this length of time.

Why hadn't he called in earlier? Had Elisabeth completely wiped everything out of his mind? He grinned at the thought. He wouldn't be at all surprised. From everything he could remember, she had mesmerized him completely. How else had she gotten him to agree to a platonic relationship when the very thought of her created all sorts of reactions within him?

He shook his head. He'd wanted to be close to her. At least he was with her at night. He wondered if he'd told her it was for her own safety? Probably not. He wouldn't want to alarm her. As far as that went, Charlie had secured this place with the most up-to-date surveillance equipment.

Tim wondered if the Barringer brothers were aware of Charlie's precautions. If not, they might have quite a surprise coming.

However, he wasn't going to underestimate them. They wouldn't be foolish enough to do anything personally. They would see that someone else took all the risks.

Sooner or later he would have to have a little brotherly talk with them. But he wanted to see what they planned to do first. In the meantime, he was going to spend as much time as possible convincing Elisabeth that their marriage would be as real and as permanent as he could make it.

The last thought he had as he settled his head on his pillow next to his sleeping bride was that he couldn't even remember the last time he'd kissed her!

Tim knew he was dreaming but he was enjoying himself too much to be concerned. He and Elisabeth were swimming in a lagoon filled with clear blue water surrounded on three sides by the gleaming white sand of a deserted beach. Palm trees swayed lazily in the breeze. Sunlight sparkled across the water and tinted her bare shoulders.

He reached for her, wanting to touch her, and she floated to him, her body nudging his. They were both as unadorned as the day they were born, but it didn't matter. They were in their own private paradise, having to share their tropical haven with no one but each other.

He tipped her chin slightly so he could kiss her, his mouth finding hers in a rush of pleasure. She seemed to melt against him, fitting her body to the contours of his. Her arms lifted to slide around his neck, which caused her breasts to nestle even closer... pressed seductively against his chest.

He could feel the tingling urgency of his body everywhere she touched him, and he quivered with need. Lifting his mouth from hers, he glanced into her face and saw the dreaming expression she wore. He knew he couldn't wait much longer to possess her. Lifting her high in his arms and holding her tightly against his chest, he waded through the water to shore, where he could place her on the soft grass in the shade of the palm trees and make delicious love to her.

He ran his hand lightly down her warm, bare body and felt her immediate response to his touch. Unerringly he bent his head and touched his tongue to the tip of her breast.

Perhaps it was her soft sigh that brought him out of his dream and caused Tim to realize that he was in fact making love to Elisabeth.

Faint moonlight flowed through the long windows, giving indistinct light to the bedroom. He could see her plainly. Her eyes were closed, but her arms were draped around his shoulders, her breasts only inches from his mouth.

He could feel his heart pounding in his chest at what was happening. When had this started, and how could he best handle it? Her lips were slightly parted, still moist from his kisses. Even while he watched her he allowed his hand to lightly slide across her abdomen down to the cluster of curls that protected her femininity.

She raised her hips to him in a coaxing movement that undid him. His fingers searched, then found what they were seeking, confirming that she wanted him, was more than ready for him.

Still more than half asleep himself, he allowed his feelings to overcome his thoughts. Once more he found her breast with his mouth and began to rhythmically tug while his fingers continued their own special brand of magic.

Elisabeth whimpered, kneading his shoulders like a kitten, lifting her hips to him in silent supplication.

With a swift movement Tim removed his briefs and moved over her. Blindly he found her mouth and possessed it in the same way he possessed her body—skillfully, tenderly and with a determination that could not be denied.

Elisabeth showed no signs of not wanting his possession. She clung to him fiercely, meeting his steady, rhythmic movements with ones of equal impatience as though she had been starved for his touch, denied of the pleasure they were finding in each other's arms.

As though they were two halves of a finely tuned whole they reached a climactic explosion together, each fiercely clinging to the other as their bodies trembled in the aftermath of their fiery ardor.

Tim felt almost boneless while he lay there. Because he had feared that his weight would be too much for her, he had rolled with her still in his arms until he lay flat on his back, with Elisabeth lying across his chest.

Neither of them had said a word to the other. It was as though both wanted to treat their tumultuous coming together as part of a moonlit dream sequence that might be shattered by a spoken word.

Tim couldn't seem to think. His body continued to pump the adrenaline and desire through him. As though disconnected from his brain, his hands yielded to the temptation of touching her soft skin, tracing from her shoulders to her hips in a yearning to memorize each curve and hollow, each texture that made her who she was.

He felt her shift slightly against him and reluctantly loosened his grasp. Lazily she touched her tongue to his neck, then delicately kissed him. Instead of pulling away, she allowed her hand to lightly flow across his chest, then down along the rigid stomach muscles, her hand gliding...soothing and yet arousing, despite their earlier fervor.

Tim turned his head slightly so his mouth rested against her forehead. He felt a fine sheen of moisture that he knew covered his body as well. He gently pressed a kiss there that began a tactile trail leading to her lips.

He felt the slight catch in her breath when he covered her mouth, leisurely exploring its depths, all the while fully aware of the sensuous pattern her fingers played across his torso.

They moved in silence and in slow motion, touching, tasting and tantalizing each other. No longer were they bound by fierce needs and unfulfilled longings. Now they had time to savor each sensation.

The tension built so slowly as to be almost nonexistent. It was as though at any time one expected to find the other had fallen asleep. Instead of sleep, however, their already sensitive bodies were feeling the increased tempo of a heartbeat, the soft exhalation of pleasure, the beginnings of urgency.

Still sprawled across him, Elisabeth slowly shifted, inch by inch, until she cradled his arousal. He lifted her slightly, just enough to enter and take possession of her once more.

Still in a dream state, they moved to an unconscious rhythm with slow thrusts and even slower withdrawals until, despite themselves, the surge of completion suddenly engulfed them, wrapping around them with a sudden greediness that insisted and persisted, casting them out of their sheltered lee into the full force of all the elements—wind, water, earth and fire.

By the time they were released from the elemental forces, both had succumbed to an even deeper sleep than that from which nature had previously aroused them. For a little while, at least, each had found a small measure of peace.

Tim woke up to bright sunlight and a sense that all was well in the best possible world. His head was clear, and he felt alert, rested and satiated. When he remembered why his eyes flew open.

He glanced at the bed. He was alone. Leaning on one elbow, he looked around the room, wondering where Elisabeth was and how long she had been gone. There were no clues. He ran his hand through his tousled hair and frowned.

Damn.

He needed to see her, preferably before they went downstairs to start their day. He needed to explain about last night, to—

Explain what? What was there to say, after all? They had needed each other, been drawn to each other, had clung to each other. Last night had been a culmination of all the stress and strain both of them had been under for weeks.

He got out of bed and started to the bathroom, wondering if she'd buy that.

The truth was that he had wanted her, had wanted her from the moment he had first laid eyes on her. He still couldn't comprehend how he had managed not to make love to her until now. But the fact was that he had, and that all the rules had been changed now.

Thank God.

They were married, and by damn they were going to stay married. He wasn't sure how he was going to convince Elisabeth of that at the moment, but he could be as stubborn as she was when he really wanted something. Now that he knew what he wanted he would be unswerving in pursuit of his goal.

She belonged to him now. She just didn't know it.

Tim was glad to have sorted all that out in his head by the time he reached the bathroom door, which opened in front of him and revealed his delectable-looking wife wearing a towel and a frown. He had a sudden compulsive need to remove both of them.

"Good morning," he said with a grin. "I was just coming to look for you."

Since he hadn't bothered covering himself Elisabeth was given an unadulterated view of her husband. She didn't appear to be overly impressed with the sight.

"Why?" After the first all-encompassing glance, her eyes remained on his. Her voice was as aloof as her gaze.

He ignored it. If anything, his grin widened. Miss Elisabeth might be able to use that cool, aloof gaze to good effect with others. In actual fact, she'd had results using it with him until now. Because now he knew the truth. Beneath that frosty facade lurked a warm and passionate woman he would never lose sight of, no matter how diligently she attempted to hide.

He leaned against the doorjamb and nonchalantly crossed one foot over the other, effectively blocking her exit from the small, steam-filled room.

"Why?" he repeated. "Because I wanted to suggest that it was much too early for us to be getting up. I'm sure you could use some more rest."

"I'm fine." Although her tone held steady, a tiny flush seemed to crawl across her cheekbones, and her gaze wavered for a moment. Just a moment, but it was enough. She wasn't nearly as composed as she would like him to believe.

"Honey, you are much more than fine. You are incomparable."

The soft color in her cheeks brightened to a crimson hue.

"Last night didn't mean a thing!"

After meeting her gaze for a moment he took a leisurely inventory of her, from the curls that were still pinned on top of her head to the wisps that had fallen around her neck and over her ears to the way the towel slightly flattened her breasts, causing them to swell above the rough material—reminding him of how they had felt the night before pressed against him—to her thighs, which were revealed by the towel wrapped around her, down the long line of her shapely legs, to her dainty ankles and feet. Without a doubt the woman was a true work of art. Tim had an urge to start at the bottom and kiss every inch of her body.

His thoughts must have been revealed on his face, he decided ruefully, as she uselessly tugged at her inadequate cover.

"Didn't it?" he murmured. "Are you sure?"

She stepped toward him as though expecting Tim to give way and allow her through the doorway. He did not live up to her expectations. She had made a tactical error in getting within arm's length of him. Never one to miss an opportunity, Tim snaked his arms around her waist and pulled her against him.

"You can't just—" was as far as Elisabeth managed to protest before his mouth found hers, effectively rebutting her statement. Obviously he could. And he did.

Tim took his time kissing her, enjoying the fact that she was determined not to give in to what was obviously between them and therefore held herself stiffly against him, her mouth primly closed. He used the time to nibble on her outthrust bottom lip, tasting it, testing its softness, letting his tongue stroke it until he was rewarded by her soft gasp as her mouth parted slightly and he gained entrance.

Somewhere in the ensuing moments, Elisabeth forgot about her towel and the necessity for keeping it firmly in place. At first her hands grasped his upper arms as though to prevent him from holding her any closer. Then, as though caught up in the play of muscles beneath her fingertips, she idly stroked the bare expanse of smooth skin stretched tautly over those same bunched muscles.

The towel shifted, slowly unfolding until her back was bare. Only the closeness between their bodies held the towel in place.

Tim didn't lift his head from hers, but continued to sip and savor her while he allowed his hands the freedom to roam across her back. She didn't seem to be aware of the moment when he lifted her in his arms and carried her into the bedroom and up the two steps to the bed. He lowered them both to the mattress.

He could not believe that anything could be more perfect than what they had shared the night before, but somehow the morning brightness seemed to enhance each movement as they clung to each other.

By the time he entered her they were both aching for completion and release, having deliberately teased and tormented and delayed their coming together until they were ready to explode.

When that internal explosion came it wiped out all memory of everything that might have come before, creating all new sensations of pleasure and release as though together they had been reborn.

Elisabeth was almost sobbing as she buried her head in Tim's shoulder, while he took long gulps of air to feed his oxygen-starved body. He couldn't begin to understand what kept happening between them. He just knew it was rare and needed to be carefully guarded, nurtured and, most important, appreciated.

They continued to lie there while he stroked her hair. He would never grow tired of touching her, holding her, expressing his need of her. He knew that. Did she?

When she finally lifted her head and looked at him he was dismayed to see tears in her eyes. The sheen made them sparkle like emeralds in the morning sunlight that filled the room.

"This doesn't change anything," she said fiercely.

"Doesn't it?" He kept his voice low and warily watched her.

"No. It just proves that we're normal, healthy human beings and that our present situation has thrown us into an intimacy that is not only understandable but expected." When he didn't comment she lifted her chin slightly and went on. "Once you're gone we'll forget everything that happened and just get on with our lives."

"Where am I going?" He asked the question with a show of interest that seemed to irritate her.

"Back to wherever you came from. Granddad is gone now. He died happy, knowing that his helpless little granddaughter was properly protected by the man of his choice."

"His choice?"

"Certainly. I knew he'd written you, even though he tried to make it seem that you just happened to be in the neighborhood. Neither one of you fooled me for a minute."

"I never tried to fool you. You were the one who told me about the letter, remember?"

"Oh, all right. Granddad tried, then."

"And you think that he wrote to ask me to rush over here and marry his helpless little granddaughter?" Tim couldn't control the laughter in his voice.

"I wouldn't put it past him."

"Could it be possible that I married you because I wanted to and for no other reason?"

"No, it couldn't."

"And why is that?"

"Because the more I've gotten to know you, the less likely it is that you were swept off your feet."

"Is that why you insisted on our having a platonic relationship?"

She glanced down, saw how closely entwined the two of them were and frowned. "We agreed," she muttered.

"But I don't remember the agreement."

Her eyes met his. "What do you remember?"

Why did he get the feeling his answer was important to her? He shrugged. "Oh, various things, some more clearly than others."

"If you remember anything at all, you will recall that you promised to leave once Granddad was gone and buried."

He wondered why she was lying. A promise of that nature would have been the last thing he would have consented to under the circumstances.

"Is that what you want?"

Her gaze shifted, and she attempted to move away. He tightened his hold on her just enough to dissuade her from her planned withdrawal.

"If we're going to argue I much prefer to do so in a horizontal position with you in my arms without any clothes on."

"We aren't going to argue. We're just going to each get on with our lives. I appreciate your being here with me these past few weeks, Tim. You and Granddad were right. But I see no reason to prolong the situation. It will only make it harder to get used to being on my own after you leave."

"You have no desire to make this a permanent relationship?"

She shook her head. "There was never any question of that. Never."

He couldn't deny that, since he didn't remember all the details. Just because he had decided he liked being married didn't mean she had reached the same conclusion.

Obviously she had no intention of continuing the relationship. Without her cooperation, what could he do about it?

Tim released her and climbed out of bed without saying a word. He walked into the bathroom and closed the door.

So much for trying to convince her that she couldn't live without him. He reached into the shower and turned on the water, then stepped under the hot spray. So much for the lonesome Lothario approach. He had to admit he didn't have any background or experience in how to convince a woman he loved her and wanted to spend the rest of his life with her.

He had a hunch he wouldn't be given a great deal of time to try to perfect his technique.

Chapter Seven

When Tim walked into the dining room he saw that Elisabeth was not alone. She was seated at the small table where Mrs. Brodie served the two of them their meals talking to a tall, lean man past his first youth. The man was dressed in expensive though battered boots, well-worn jeans and a work shirt that had seen multiple washings. He was twisting a Stetson around by the brim. Tim decided the man must be Sam, the ranch foreman.

He soon found that his guess had been correct.

"Tim, Sam's just told me that several head of cattle disappeared last night. The men found tracks that looked as though they were hauled out by a large tractor-trailer rig."

Tim motioned to a third chair as he sat. "Sit down, Sam, and have some coffee so I can enjoy mine. My brain works considerably quicker after I've had a cup or two."

Sam seemed more at ease once Tim joined them, and Tim recognized him to be one of a certain breed of man who isn't comfortable around women, particularly if the woman happens to be his new boss.

Tim listened as Elisabeth plied Sam with a multitude of questions, some of which Sam could only answer with a guess.

Elisabeth immediately caught the implications. "It's because Charlie is gone, isn't it? Somebody's letting me know I can't just expect things to go on as they were."

"Maybe not, ma'am. There's always a certain amount of rustling that goes on in cattle country. We've probably gotten a little lax around here lately because there hasn't been much sign of it in these parts for several months. That's my fault. I'll do everything I can to see that the cattle are recovered."

"You've notified the sheriff?" Tim asked quietly.

Sam nodded. "First thing this morning. He said he'd be out as soon as he could to see what he could pick up."

Mrs. Brodie brought in their breakfast. Sam refused anything to eat and promised to let them know if there was any more information, then left.

"What do you think?" Elisabeth said after Tim had allowed the silence to continue between them.

"About what?"

She just stared at him until he grinned. Something in his eyes caused her to drop her gaze and fiddle with the handle of her cup.

"You're right," she said in a low voice. "It's really none of your business what happens around here. I know that."

He shook his head. "Anything that concerns you will always be my business, Elisabeth, regardless of whether I continue to stay here or accept your edict and leave. I can't argue with you about our reasons for getting married or any agreements the two of us made when Charlie wasn't around. All I have to go by is my own feelings. And I feel committed to you. After last night I feel even more committed."

"That's what I was afraid of!" she cried. "That's why I didn't want us to make love. I didn't want anything to trigger that macho condition in you that would make you feel obligated to me."

"I don't feel obligated. I'm here because I want to be."

"Nonsense. You're here because Charlie got his own way again."

Tim grinned. "The man wasn't God, you know. He couldn't control everything."

"He did a great imitation of thinking he could, though."

Tim reached over and placed his hand on hers and felt her quiver at his touch. "Everything's going to be all right, Elisabeth. Let's just give it some time, all right?"

They sat there looking into each other's eyes. Tim could see the uncertainty and the pain in hers. He hoped she could see the concern and caring in his.

"What are your plans for today?" he finally asked.

She moved her hands to her lap. "I thought I would try to do a little writing."

"Anything in particular?"

He could almost see her withdrawing into herself. "Oh, just the usual scribbling I always do to entertain myself, as Granddad always used to say."

"Do you find it helps to write?"

"Yes," she responded coolly. "I often find that I like the people I write about a great deal more than the ones I'm around."

"Ouch." He leaned back in his chair and studied her. The warm, vibrant woman he had known was gone. In her place was the lady filled with pride who was fiercely independent. Well, he would allow her that pride and independence because he knew he could do nothing to change it. He understood both traits, having an abundant amount of his own.

If she didn't want him, he would accept her decision. He didn't have to like it, he just had to accept it. He also had to keep his promise to Charlie.

Rising, he nodded to her and said, "If you'll excuse me, I have some calls to make."

"Aren't you leaving this morning?"

"I know how eager you are to get rid of me, but there are a few details that Charlie asked me to take care of. I'll try to complete them as quickly as possible and get out of your hair." He left the room quickly, closing his mind to their situation.

He still had a job to do. He'd deal with how he felt later.

The first call he made was to Greg's office. Tim was relieved to learn that Greg was in.

Greg answered his phone by saying, "Is this really the Tim Walker I used to know, the one I haven't heard from in so long I've forgotten what he looks like?"

"Don't get smart."

"It certainly sounds like my old buddy, Timothy. How've you been?"

"Busy. Is it too late to celebrate Cindy's birthday?"

"Certainly not. Her first one has come and gone, of course. You know how time flies. But she's graduating from college now and we're going to throw a big bash that you're welcome to attend."

"Cute, Duncan. Really cute. How does Brandi put up with you?"

"She has a much better sense of humor than you do, I suppose. Where'd you misplace yours?"

Tim sighed and ran his hand through his hair. "Good question."

Greg's voice sobered. "Problems?"

"You could say that."

"Anything I can do to help?"

"Do you have any idea how relieved I am to hear you offer? Yeah, I could use some help."

"Name it."

"Is there a chance you could come to Colorado for a few days?"

"When?"

"As soon as you can get away."

"Alone?"

"Yeah."

"Denver or the cabin?"

"Neither. Cripple Creek."

There was a long silence. "Cripple Creek?" drawled Greg.

"I'm staying at Charlie Barringer's place. Have you been here?"

"No, but I suppose I could find it. Didn't I just read somewhere that he'd passed away?"

"The funeral was yesterday. He left a few things he wanted to have cleared up. I'd feel a hell of a lot better if I had you around to guard my back."

"Hold on. Let me check my calendar."

Tim doodled on the writing pad that had been placed on the desk, drawing squares, rectangles, circles with arrows pointing from one to the other.

"I think I can rearrange things so I could leave early tomorrow morning. That should put me there by dark."

"Thanks." Tim gave Greg directions, then said, "I suppose I'd better explain something before you get here. I'm, uh, married to Elisabeth Barringer, Charlie's granddaughter."

An explosive silence greeted him.

"Married?" Greg finally whispered as though the breath had been knocked out of him.

"At least temporarily," Tim added grudgingly. "I'll try to explain when you get here. It's all a little confusing at the moment."

"Do you want Brandi to know? She's going to be devastated that you didn't tell us sooner."

"I'd thought of that. If you don't mind, I'd rather you didn't. As soon as I get this matter cleared up, there may be nothing to tell her."

"We'll talk," Greg said quietly. "It sounds like you need to. I've never known you to do anything so out of character as to jump into a marriage with someone you don't know." He paused. "Or am I assuming wrong about your just having met her?"

"Your assumption is correct."

"Hang in there. I'm on my way."

Tim managed a grin. "The cavalry to the rescue. Just like old times, right?"

"I'll see you," Greg replied, ignoring the reference to the fact that Greg had once saved Tim's life when they'd been in the service. That was how they had met. Tim had never forgotten, and Greg always refused to discuss it.

After he hung up, Tim sat for a few moments, then decided to find Sam and wait for the sheriff. He had to do something, keep his mind occupied, keep the thought of Elisabeth at bay. That was the only way he knew to survive.

Tim spent the following hours riding with Sam in his Jeep, going over possible places to enter the ranch that were isolated enough for rustlers to risk coming on the property.

They agreed to hire extra help to spell the regular hands during off-duty hours. While they were checking the area, Sam obligingly pointed out the spot where Tim had been found a few days before.

Tim acknowledged to himself that he hadn't really believed Charlie's concerns were valid until he'd been attacked. He would not be careless again. He and Sam got out and walked the area, looking for signs that others had been there recently. The signs weren't hard to spot, as though the men who had made them hadn't been concerned with early detection.

Tim explained to Sam what he thought was happening and why, and accepted his offer of help when the time came. Now, more than ever, Tim knew that Charlie had accurately judged Jason and Marcus.

He found it strange how money and power affected some people. For some there was never enough. Since Charlie had been so concerned, Tim had assumed that he was leaving most of his estate to Elisabeth, which would naturally create an aggressive fight. Neil, his attorney, had pointed out that Charlie had known better. By evenly disbursing his estate, Charlie knew that no judge would consider throwing out the will when the only reason for contesting it was spite. In monetary value, Elisabeth had only received her due.

Tim's job was to make sure that she was allowed to live in peace.

He thought of her questions about his job and how she had suggested that he might be an IRS agent. Perhaps it was an idea he could utilize. There was more than one way to get a person's attention, after all.

Tim made a note to call Max when he returned to the house.

Elisabeth sat at the computer in the room she had converted into an office and stared out the window. She had used a need to write as an excuse to closet herself away from everyone. Mrs. Brodie knew not to disturb her until she decided to come out. Even her grandfather had always respected her need to be left alone.

Her grandfather.

She sighed, restlessly getting up. He seemed to be the basis of everything that was happening to her. At least her strong feelings for him seemed to control her behavior.

How had she allowed herself to be caught up in such a situation?

As far back as she could remember, Elisabeth had been taught by her mother that a woman had to be strong, that she had only herself to rely on, that sometimes emotions could betray a woman, causing her to make foolish choices.

Invariably her mother used herself as an example. She had been in her early twenties, living in Tucson, earning an adequate living working in an office, when she'd met Elisabeth's father. He'd had an appointment to see Cathy's boss regarding some real estate. She had been flattered by his attention and accepted his invitation to dinner that night.

Cathy had never been able to explain to Elisabeth how she could have known so quickly that Chuck Barringer was the man she wanted to have in her life. Since meeting Tim, Elisabeth could better understand her mother's reaction. Elisabeth had discovered the lack of control she had over her own emotions the day she'd walked into her grandfather's hospital room and seen Tim for the first time. Even now she couldn't begin to understand the thunderbolt experience it had been. Was it because of some hereditary flaw she and her mother carried that all their logical thinking processes disappeared when a certain type of male appeared in their lives?

Her mother had only been able to shake her head, unable to find the words to explain what had happened. Elisabeth could only accept that from their first evening together, Cathy and Chuck had known that something momentous had happened between them and that it was too important to ignore.

Chuck had been honest about his situation. He and his wife were separated. Because of his wife's family, background and concern for social standing, she would not consider divorce.

None of that had mattered to Cathy. They had discussed the implications of a possible pregnancy. As much as Chuck had wanted to father a child of Cathy's, they had known it was impractical and unfair and had taken precautions to ensure that she would not become pregnant.

Because of the papers he carried, she had been one of the first people to be notified of his unexpected death. Even now Elisabeth could see her mother's face whenever she talked about that time in her life. Death was the only eventuality neither of them had planned for.

Cathy had quit her job so she could travel with Chuck. She had planned to go with him when he went to Europe, but at the last minute she became ill, and Chuck had had to go without her. Had she been with him, she might have died as well. Elisabeth had a hunch that Cathy might have wished for such a fate.

But then her mother's face would light up as she told the next part of her story. How the illness that had prevented her from traveling with Chuck had not gotten better. That the news of his death had seemed to worsen her physical condition. That finally, knowing she had to get some help to get back on her feet, she went to the doctor, and he had told her she was pregnant.

She wouldn't believe it. They had used birth control. How had it happened? The doctor had explained that nothing was one hundred percent foolproof. The fact remained that despite everything, she was going to have a part of Chuck after all. Elisabeth became Cathy's miracle baby.

Elisabeth smiled at the memory. She had many happy memories of her mother. Cathy had wasted no time finding a place where she could have a child and raise it. She had devoted her life to raising Elisabeth.

Cathy had loved her little daughter. She'd laughed when no one believed Elisabeth belonged to her because she looked just like her father. Cathy's hair had been dark, her eyes gray, and she had been petite. Elisabeth knew from a picture she'd seen of him that she looked like her father. She really hadn't cared, as long as her mother didn't mind.

Elisabeth always listened to Cathy's stories about her love for Chuck, the choices she had made and the joy of having Elisabeth in her life. But in Elisabeth's mind she had perceived the problem Cathy would never point out: You can't count on love. You can only count on yourself. Things happen. People leave you, sometimes not because they want to, but because life works that way.

Cathy had proven Elisabeth's theory to her by dying when Elisabeth was still so young.

At fourteen, Elisabeth had known that she was capable of looking after herself and had been determined to prove it. That was when Charles Barringer barged into her life and demanded the right to look after her.

She smiled at the memory. Granddad was a great one for demanding. He'd wanted to take her home with him, wrap her up in tissue and soft cotton and have her do nothing for the rest of her life, protected from the world.

He had been too late to change who she was and how she dealt with life. Most surprising of all, he had accepted her. Oh, he had enjoyed battling with her, more for the fun of the argument than that he had any desire to win. He'd enjoyed crossing swords with her, but had always fought fair.

Until now.

Bringing Tim Walker into her life when she was at her most vulnerable had been a sneaky, underhanded thing to do to her. And he had known it. How, she didn't know, but her grandfather had known. She'd seen the look of delight on his face at her reaction to Tim.

How could he have done this to her? All her careful plans, her sensible views about life and herself, her ability to think logically and practically had immediately dissipated like puffs of smoke in a sudden wind.

Would it have made any difference to her if Tim had been a stranger to her grandfather as well as to her? Probably not, she decided honestly. After that first few hours together, when it seemed as though they had always known each other, she was ready to place her heart in his hands.

She had done just that. She knew that Tim now believed she had only married him to please her grandfather. She was eager to grasp at that particular straw in an effort to give herself time to evaluate what was happening to her.

After he was hurt, she had been determined to distance herself from him. During his memory loss he had made it clear that marriage wasn't a part of his life-style.

She had known and understood that. Hadn't she felt the same way? Until she met Tim, of course.

Elisabeth understood herself a little better. It wasn't that she didn't love Tim or that she didn't need Tim; she didn't want to need him. She wanted to stay invulnerable to hurt.

Losing her grandfather had been a reminder, if she had needed one, about the pain of loving, then losing, someone.

Turning back to her manuscript, Elisabeth felt relief that at least she had her make-believe world she could escape to whenever life became too consuming for her. Thank God she had gained some level of professional security in her chosen field.

Thinking of her career reminded her of the argument she and Tim had had the day he had been hurt. He had come looking for her, too impatient to wait for her to surface. He had seen the letter from her editor, as well as the royalty statements that had arrived, which she had neglected to put away. Elisabeth hadn't expected anyone to come into her office and had grown careless.

She had gotten angry at Tim's questions, angrier still that he should criticize her decision not to share her success with her grandfather. She had reacted by becoming defensive, until they were both shouting. It had been a silly argument in some ways, but it pointed to the heart of her dilemma. She had spent too many years keeping people at a distance. Her reasons for not sharing her professional success with her grandfather had been based on the knowledge that he would not really appreciate what she was doing, and she didn't want him to ridicule her efforts.

Perhaps she'd had something of the same feelings about Tim finding out. As it happened, she never learned his reaction. By the time she was able to talk to him again, he had no memory of discovering her secret.

Elisabeth realized she was hoping he would leave before all his memories returned. Making love with him had been a mistake. It had merely served to strengthen her resolve about the relationship. She was weak around him, without willpower. She couldn't take much more.

The sooner he left the better. Eventually she would be able to get on with her life alone. She didn't want to consider the fact that it might be too late. The damage had been done.

Chapter Eight

Dinner that night was strained, although each of them took pains to be polite. Elisabeth's thoughts kept returning to the time when they would go upstairs and once again share a bed. Why had she thought they could sleep together and not be drawn to each other? But she had wanted to be near him, particularly once he'd been injured. After the doctor explained that there was little that could be done except to allow him time to heal, she had insisted he be kept at the house.

She had cherished those hours with him. She had spent the time sitting beside him, watching him, studying him and, when he murmured disjointedly, discovering how her calm voice and soothing touch seemed to comfort him.

She had also wanted to let him know that she had finally agreed with him about her work. The next time she'd been to see her grandfather, she'd told him the truth about her career. He hadn't been as surprised as she expected. He was very proud of her for showing the initiative and stubbornness to stick with it.

When Tim had awakened not recognizing her she had been shocked, unsure of how to handle the situation. She and her grandfather had disagreed about what she should do, but then they had disagreed about most things.

Sometimes she was convinced her grandfather argued just for the sake of being contrary.

Elisabeth glanced across the table at the silent man who filled her thoughts. She wondered what he was thinking but didn't feel she had a right to ask.

Tim's thoughts kept returning to Greg's upcoming visit. He reviewed his plans. He thought he had covered all the bases, but only time would tell. Now if Jason and Marcus would only step into the carefully baited trap, the matter would be taken care of shortly.

Then what? What more could he say to Elisabeth? He supposed he wasn't being fair to her. After all, she agreed to the marriage as a temporary measure. Did he have any right to demand that the rules be changed?

Was it her fault he had fallen so hard for her that he didn't want to think about a future she wasn't a part of?

"Will there be anything else?"

Tim and Elisabeth were startled by the sound of Mrs. Brodie's voice breaking into the silence that surrounded them.

Elisabeth was first to respond. "No, thank you, Mrs. Brodie. Everything was delicious."

Mrs. Brodie looked at their plates, then at the two people sitting there. "How would you know? Doesn't look like either one of you bothered to eat a thing."

For the first time since they'd sat down, each became aware of the other's mood and lack of conversation. They put their own interpretation on it.

Tim decided that Elisabeth was still upset with him for not having left. Elisabeth assumed Tim was irritated that she was still insisting that he leave. Since each felt justified in their position, there was nothing to be said.

When Elisabeth stood, Tim also got up. "If you will excuse me, I have some things to take care of."

She nodded. He disappeared into the library, and she slowly went upstairs, feeling drained. Perhaps she would go to bed early and try to get some rest. Tonight she would use some common sense and wear her gown to bed.

The memory of going to sleep the night before with his hands stroking and smoothing the muscles of her back and shoulders popped into her mind. She hadn't intended to fall asleep and was, in fact, surprised she did under the circumstances. But she had been under a great deal of strain, and his touch had been so gentle and soothing.

Later she had come awake to find him touching her in a new and more urgent way. She could no more have resisted him than she could have admitted to him how much she loved him. Her longing for him had worked against her.

She couldn't allow herself that weakness again.

Tim called Max and explained his idea about the brothers Barringer. In the long run, he felt his idea would work even better than bringing formal charges against them. Once he made them aware that he knew what they were up to, he needed a permanent lever to make sure they didn't harass Elisabeth.

Max laughed at his idea, but agreed that it would probably work.

Then Tim sat in the big overstuffed chair and thought about Elisabeth upstairs. Glancing at his watch, he was surprised to see how late it was. Maybe he'd be able to sleep. He hoped so. And he hoped to hell he wouldn't dream!

Tim heard Greg's car pull in the driveway the next evening and was outside by the time his friend got out of the car.

"You made good time," he said, greeting Greg with a warm handshake.

"I got an early start." Greg glanced around and gave a low whistle. "Quite a place."

"I know. It takes some getting used to."

"It looks more like a movie set than a working ranch."

"The ranching part is to utilize the land, not to make the place a paying concern."

Greg removed his suitcase from the trunk of the car and followed Tim to the front door.

"I guess you know you've been more than a little mysterious, my friend. Care to fill me in on what's been going on in your life?"

"I have every intention of doing so after dinner and once we're alone."

"Is your wife here?"

Tim held the door open for Greg. When Greg walked inside his question was answered. He saw the blond, green-eyed beauty standing in the foyer, a hesitant smile on her lips.

"You must be Greg," she said softly. "Tim has told me so much about you."

"And you're Elisabeth," he replied with a grin. Setting down his suitcase, he quickly covered the distance between the two of them and clasped her outstretched hand in both of his. "I'm sorry to say that Tim hasn't told me nearly enough about you, which is an omission I'm not sure I'm ready to forgive him for."

The man standing before her was several inches taller than Tim and not as broad. His blond hair was touched with gray and gave him a distinguished appearance that made her immediately feel comfortable with him.

"You must be tired if you made that drive today. Why don't we have coffee? Dinner should be ready in fifteen minutes or so."

Tim picked up the suitcase. "I'll take this upstairs. Your room is the first one at the top of the stairs. You shouldn't have any trouble finding it."

Greg took in the sumptuous foyer, the polished mahogany railing of the stairway, the gleaming marble floor, and shook his head.

Elisabeth grinned at his expression. "I know. It's really too much, isn't it? I feel as though I should be wearing full skirts with a multitude of petticoats and other unmentionables every time I come down the stairs.''

She led him into the front room and motioned for him to have a seat. Mrs. Brodie appeared in the doorway and Elisabeth asked for coffee, then sank onto the sofa across from Greg.

''I'm sure this place has some stories it could tell. How old is it?''

''My grandfather said that his father built it just before the turn of the century. He was one of the fortunate ones who discovered gold in the area, and he wanted a home befitting his new station in life.''

''Yes, I remember hearing once that the Cripple Creek area had one of the last big gold rushes in the United States.''

Elisabeth nodded. ''In the 1890s Cripple Creek was a flourishing metropolis. Now there's just a small community left. The principal source of income is tourism.'' She glanced around the room, then at Greg. ''I find the history of that era fascinating.''

Greg watched the woman seated across from him and tried to come to terms with the fact that she was Tim's wife. Somehow he had thought that Tim would never marry. Of course he had thought the same thing about himself a few years ago, and look at him now.

''How long have you and Tim been married?'' Only when he heard his question did Greg realize he'd voiced his thoughts. He was embarrassed with his bluntness. Fortunately Tim walked into the room and rescued him. Greg hoped he hadn't sounded to

Elisabeth as though he were interrogating a helpless witness.

"Almost a month ago, although I only recall the last few days," Tim replied. He sat beside Elisabeth and casually took her hand. Greg wondered about the tension he sensed between the two of them. His curiosity grew by the minute.

"Yes, you mentioned something about getting a blow to your head. How are you feeling?"

"Much better. The pain's almost gone, and my memory is returning—" he glanced at Elisabeth as he drawled the rest of his statement "—slowly but surely."

Greg could see her stiffen slightly. Glancing at Tim, he asked, "Did you find out how it happened?"

"It was just a careless accident on my part," Tim replied, with a slight shake of his head. "I haven't been on horseback in years."

Greg lifted a brow, but felt it safer not to comment. He was relieved when Mrs. Brodie came in to tell them that dinner was ready to be served.

Having Greg at the evening meal livened up the conversation and eased the tension for everyone. He shared hilarious stories about his children, and he and Tim regaled Elisabeth with stories about Brandi, as she was now as a wife and mother and years before, when she was growing up.

At one point Elisabeth said, "I'm so sorry she wasn't able to come with you to visit us." Greg threw Tim a questioning glance, which Tim returned without expression.

"Yes, she was, too," Greg responded in a bland tone. "Maybe next time," then wondered why Tim and Elisabeth would not look at each other.

By the time Elisabeth excused herself for the evening Greg was ready to throttle Tim if necessary to get some answers.

"I wish to hell I understood what was going on around here," he said once the two men were alone.

Tim poured them both a drink, then sat down across from his friend. "I appreciate the delicacy with which you handled the matter. Now you can see why I didn't dare have Brandi come with you."

Greg grinned, acknowledging the accuracy of Tim's hit. "Brandi has never been known for her tact and diplomacy. She would have been asking questions and demanding answers before we had gotten inside the house."

Tim leaned his head against the back of the chair and stretched his legs in front of him. "I hope Brandi wasn't too upset about not coming with you."

Greg took a sip of his drink and gave a brief sigh of pleasure. "Of course she wasn't. Brandi's mature and understanding." He glanced at Tim, his eyes sparkling. "And I didn't tell her that my unexpected business meeting was with you."

Tim began to laugh, and Greg joined him.

"You've learned a great deal about married life," Tim said after a moment. "I wonder if I'll be given that chance."

"Meaning?"

"Elisabeth is already asking when I plan to leave."

"I could think of many reasons she might want to send you packing. What is hers?"

Tim looked into his drink, then took a swallow. "Because, according to her, we agreed to marry as a temporary measure to please her grandfather."

"I had no idea you were so self-sacrificing. A beautiful, intelligent, wealthy young woman needs a spouse, and you quickly offer to help her out. How noble."

Tim toasted his friend. "I knew you would understand."

Greg slid down a few inches in his chair and propped his feet on the footstool in front of him, and Tim got up to freshen their drinks. After handing Greg his drink Tim began to fill Greg in on everything he could remember. When he finished, Greg shook his head.

"You are a source of constant amazement, my friend. How do you always manage to get in the thick of things?"

"Just my natural talent, I suppose," Tim offered modestly.

"So what's going on with Elisabeth's brothers now?"

"Half-brothers."

Greg waved his hand as though brushing away a pesky fly. "Whatever."

"According to Charlie, Jason visited him not long after Charlie was hospitalized to talk about the possibilities of reopening the gold mine located on the ranch."

Greg straightened slightly from his relaxed position and stared at Tim. "Elisabeth mentioned something earlier about a gold mine her great-grandfather owned."

"One and the same. Charlie said the mine was quite successful for years, but by the 1920s was barely breaking even, due to some problems with water seepage and a drop in gold prices. So his father closed it."

"Is it worth reopening?"

Tim thought over what he'd been told. "That's the big question at the moment. Geologists say that despite the millions of dollars worth of gold taken out of the area originally, there's an estimated eighty percent still to be recovered in the granite terrain." Leaning forward, he placed his elbows on his knees and held his glass between his fingers. "With new mining technology and the price of gold these days, reopening some of the existing mines has become an option to consider." He drained his glass and looked over at his friend. "I understand that a few of the mines around here have opened with varying degrees of success."

"I see."

Tim went to the bar and poured another drink. When he motioned with the bottle, Greg joined him, his thoughts caught up in the conversation.

"What Charlie realized when Jason visited him," Tim went on after they had reseated themselves, "was that Jason automatically assumed he and Marcus would inherit the ranch. They never gave Elisabeth a thought. What they wanted was Charlie's approval to go ahead and have the mine studied for its present mining potential. They were already looking toward the future when Charlie wouldn't be around."

"But Charlie left the ranch to Elisabeth, I take it?"

"Yes. He'd had his will drawn up several years before and saw no reason to change it. Both men lived in the East and never came out here. He and Elisabeth considered this place home. However, he could see the potential for conflict once he was gone."

Once more comfortably draped in his chair, Greg asked, "How does Elisabeth feel about all this?"

"That's the hell of it. Elisabeth doesn't know about the new interest in the mine. Charlie didn't want her worried about it. Or worse, he didn't want her turning the place over to the brothers upon demand."

"So that's where you come in, I take it."

"Supposedly, yeah. In case they need some convincing to leave her alone."

"I don't see any reason you had to marry her, though."

Tim's smile was filled with self-mockery. "My reasons for marrying her were much more basic than that. They were very territorial, in fact." He swirled the liquid in his glass. "I wanted her to belong to me, so I used the situation for my own reasons."

"How caveman of you. I've always known you lacked a certain amount of civility in your nature, but I must admit you've surprised me."

"Unfortunately, Elisabeth isn't buying any of this."

"Good for her."

"Whose side are you on, anyway?"

Greg lifted his brows in mock astonishment. "Why, I'm always on the side of truth and justice, where else?"

Tim shook his head.

"Does she know how you feel about her?"

Tim thought about that question for a long time before he answered. "It's all so complicated. From what I remember about our first meeting and the subsequent marriage arrangements, I was sure she did." He stood and began to pace the floor. "The damnable part is that I only have vague recollections of the ceremony. Then things are hazy. I'm not sure what is a dream and what's real." He paused, his hands on his hips, and frowned at Greg. "Then, a few mornings ago, I woke up with what I thought was a monster hangover pounding in my head in a strange bed with a woman I could have sworn I'd never seen before."

Greg knew this was serious, but the picture Tim painted was too humorous not to laugh. Tim's reluctant grin acknowledged that he understood Greg's amusement.

"Just think how Elisabeth must have felt to have her new husband look at her one morning and say, 'My God, who are you?'"

"Yes, I know. Charlie pointed that out to me. Since then, she's been polite but kept her distance." *Most of the time,* he added silently.

He refused to feel guilty about what had happened between them the other night. She had been too responsive, too open to his advances for him to feel that he had taken advantage of her.

"So what are you going to do?"

"About Elisabeth? I don't know. As for the mine, some of the ranch hands are keeping an eye on the area. I think Jason's going to try something soon. There's been some activity already. If he thinks his efforts will go undetected, I suspect he'll see what's down there. If it's worth it to him, he may decide to convince Elisabeth not to keep the place." He explained about the missing cattle. "I think he could very well be behind that, hoping to discourage her."

"So you intend to discourage him from discouraging her, is that it?"

"Close enough."

"And where do I come in?"

"As a witness, for one thing. If you're willing, I would also like you to go with me to visit Jason at his office in New York."

"When?"

"Soon. Within the next couple of days, if I've figured Jason correctly."

Greg was quiet for a few minutes, and Tim relaxed once more in his chair. He needed some rest. He hadn't gotten much sleep the night before. He thought of Elisabeth in bed upstairs and wondered why he thought he'd be able to sleep any better tonight.

Greg stretched and looked at his friend. "Yes. I think I'd like to be dealt into this hand. It might be fun."

"I appreciate it."

Greg lifted his brow slightly. "Oh, you'll pay for it."

"How do you mean?"

"You're going to be given the pleasure of telling Brandi that you got married without telling her. After the fuss you made when she and I snuck off, she's not going to take your doing the same thing lightly.''

Tim rose and switched off the lamp by his elbow. The men turned toward the hallway. ''If I had my say,'' Tim said as he checked the lock on the front door, ''I'd be more than willing to have another ceremony that included you and Brandi. All we have to do is to convince Elisabeth.''

''You can always explain that your friends insist. I'm sure she would understand.''

They walked up the stairs together and paused in the doorway of Greg's room. Tim rested his hand on Greg's shoulder. ''I'll do what I can. But I can't promise anything.''

''Nonsense. I've never known you to give up on something you wanted in your life, Tim. You aren't about to give up now.''

Tim grinned. ''You know me well.'' He started down the hallway to join his wife for what was left of the night.

Chapter Nine

Tim silently opened the bedroom door and slipped inside. Elisabeth had left a small nightlight on in the bathroom, and it gave off enough light for him to see the shadowy shape of furniture and her still form lying asleep in the mammoth bed they shared.

Without haste he removed his clothes and quietly joined her. He smiled when he saw the demure gown she wore. He wondered if she thought he found her less enticing dressed in her soft cotton. How little she understood that it was her, who she was, that created such a riot of feeling within him at times that he felt almost choked with its intensity.

Her very independence, her need to be self-reliant, her refusal to cave in when the odds were against her, were all qualities Tim found endearing. He loved her strength of character and her integrity. He loved all the qualities that made up the package so delectably and attractively known as Elisabeth Barringer Walker.

Unable to resist being close to her, he moved until his body was only inches away from hers. She lay on her side, facing him. With trembling fingers he smoothed a strand of hair away from her cheek.

She stirred, murmuring something that sounded like, ''Tim?''

''I'm sorry. I didn't intend to wake you,'' he whispered.

She shifted her leg, grazing him, and her lashes fluttered. ''What time is it?''

At least that's what he assumed she mumbled. He smiled, drawing her closer against him and nuzzling her neck.

''Late. Very late.''

''Mmm,'' she replied, burrowing deeper into his embrace. ''You okay?'' she said after a moment. He heard the concern in her voice, something she wouldn't allow herself when she was fully awake. Now she was operating on instinct, without her guard in place.

He followed the curve of her back and hips with his hand, pressing her body more intimately against his. ''Now I am.'' He nibbled at her ear. ''I've missed you.''

''Mmm.'' She sleepily pressed her lips against his cheek in response.

''Do you have any idea how much I love you?'' he whispered, trailing kisses across her jaw and down her neck.

She touched the back of his head with her hand and slowly caressed the thick hair there, but made no response.

"I want to marry you, Elisabeth. I want you to know how much I want you in my life. I don't want there ever to be any mistake about that." He raised his head and kissed her on the lips, and she responded by wrapping her arms tighter around him.

"Will you marry me?"

He felt her body jolt as though she'd just received a shock, as though she was finally awake for the first time since he'd come to bed. She stiffened and pulled away so she could see his face. Touching his cheek worriedly, she asked, "Tim, are you all right?"

He smiled. "I'm fine. Why?"

"Has your memory gone again?"

"No."

"Why would you ask me to marry you?" she asked, concerned.

"Because you seem in such a hurry to end our present relationship. I wanted to make it clear that I still want to be a part of your life."

He could feel her relax against him once more as though she found his words reassuring on some deep level. Tim slid his hand under her knee and pulled it over his thigh.

"Tim?"

"Yes, love."

"What are you doing?"

He smiled at the lack of concern in her voice. She was still more than half asleep. "Making love to you."

"I don't think that's a very good idea."

He kissed her, then said, "I think it's an excellent idea. I think it's the best idea I've had in hours... possibly days."

"Tim?"

"Hmm?"

"Have you been drinking?"

"A little brandy, that's all."

He kissed her again. She responded, which encouraged him immensely.

"I don't want to love you, you know," she said, her voice as soft as a young child's.

Since she was running her hands across his shoulders and back, her body pressed provocatively against him and was returning his kisses, he wasn't unduly alarmed by her comment.

"Why not?" he asked lazily, shifting so that he could open the front of her gown and caress her breasts with his mouth and tongue.

"I'm afraid," she admitted softly.

"Of me?"

"Of being hurt, of being alone, of caring too much to survive without you."

He straightened and kissed her again—slowly and with gentle thoroughness. "You don't have to be alone, sweetheart. Don't you know that yet? I'm here. I'll be here for as long as you want me." Tim lay propped above her, resting on his forearms, which he placed on either side of her head.

The light caught the glitter of her eyes, and he leaned over her and kissed each eyelid softly, reverently. "I love you, Elisabeth," he whispered.

"Oh, Tim, please don't say that. I can't bear it. Not now. It's too soon."

"Too soon to know or too soon to admit it?"

She shook her head, and moisture slid from beneath her closed eyelids. He kissed each tear away.

"Don't be afraid, love. Don't let fear rule your life. Don't push me away."

There were no more words between them. He showed her his love in physical form, reverently expressing all that he was feeling. At one point she sat up and helped him remove her gown, then turned toward him once again.

It was almost dawn before they fell asleep, exhausted, in each other's arms. Even as his eyes closed Tim realized that Elisabeth had never given him the answer he wanted from her.

Tim felt as though he'd only been asleep for a few minutes when the phone rang. This time he was closest to it. Fumbling for the receiver he snagged it with two fingers and brought it to his ear.

"H'lo?"

"Mr. Walker, this is Sam. We've got company."

"Thanks. I'll be right there."

He was out of bed by the time he'd returned the phone to its resting place.

"Who was that?" Elisabeth murmured.

"Sam. I asked him to call me early this morning. I'd forgotten when I came to bed last night."

She raised her head and looked at him. "Why?"

"I wanted to get an early start. There are some things I wanted to check out that can only be done in the early hours."

"Oh."

"Go back to sleep, love."

"You didn't get much sleep, either," she pointed out.

He grinned. "It was worth it. Believe me." He leaned over and gave her a hard, swift kiss, then backed away before he lost his will to resist.

This was the signal he'd been waiting for, gearing up for. Now things would begin to move, and he could get on with his efforts to woo Elisabeth to his way of thinking.

A few minutes later he tapped on Greg's door and opened it. "We've got company, Greg. I knew they'd show up."

Greg sat up and stretched. "They picked a hell of an hour to come visiting," he grumbled, coming to his feet.

Tim laughed. He could feel the adrenaline moving through him. "I don't think they intended to disturb us."

Greg was already dressing, his movements economical. "Thoughtful of them."

"Without a doubt. Also very considerate. I hope they'll have the information that would have taken us several months to obtain."

He went out the door with Greg close on his heels. Tim turned on a pocket flashlight so Greg could see the stairs, but kept it on only long enough for them to make it down the stairs before switching it off. He didn't want to alert anyone who might be watching the house that people were stirring.

The sky was still black and filled with stars when they stepped outside. Because of the altitude and the early hour they could see their breath when they breathed.

Tim saw a movement in the shadows, then Sam stepped away from his Jeep. The men joined him without a word. They rode for several minutes in silence before Tim asked, "Did you see how many there were?"

"Jess counted four before he sent one of the men to get me up. Jess knows not to let himself be known to them unless they try to leave before we get there."

They parked the Jeep a fair distance from the entrance of the mine, making allowances for the way the night air carried sounds. They moved swiftly and silently through the night, all three men trained in stalking. When they were within shouting distance of the mine, Jess stepped out from behind a group of boulders to meet them.

Only then did Tim realize that he could see the surrounding area. The sky had begun to lighten in the east. It wouldn't be long before dawn.

"They haven't made any real effort to be quiet, Sam," Jess pointed out. "They brought in a couple of trucks and some kind of equipment and disappeared into the mine."

Sam looked at Tim, waiting for instructions.

"How many men do you have here with you, Jess?" Tim asked.

"Six."

"Armed?"

He nodded. "Rifles."

"Fine. Have them stay out of sight of the mine entrance, but make sure it's surrounded. When I give the signal I want all of them to show themselves. There won't be any shooting, if I've read the situation correctly. These are engineers, hired to do a job. I'm just using you guys to impress on them and the man who hired them that I mean business."

Sam and Jess nodded and melted into the shadows around them.

"Now what?" Greg placed his hands at his waist and leaned back, stretching. He sounded as though he could fall asleep. Obviously he wasn't being affected by an adrenaline high, Tim thought with a smile. Either that, or he wasn't going to admit it.

"We wait. You can always go curl up in the Jeep if you want to get some more sleep."

The brief flash of a smile answered him. "Oh, I think I can manage to stay awake if you can."

Thinking back over the past few hours, Tim acknowledged that he probably hadn't had much more than an hour's sleep. But it had been worth the lack of sleep to find Elisabeth so responsive in his arms. Her feelings ran deep, he knew, much deeper than she was willing to admit. But surely after last night she could no longer ignore the intangible tie that bound them so strongly together.

Tim lost track of time as they waited. Neither man spoke but were content to share the early morning view of the mountains. They watched a doe with her fawns tiptoe through the meadow nearby on their way to an unseen stream that could be heard in the stillness. Other wildlife went on with their morning routines, ignorant of the human eyes watching them.

The sound of men's voices and boots scrambling over rocks was an unwelcome intrusion in the pastoral quiet. Tim moved closer to the entrance, waiting in the shadows of the sentinel-like pines that stood nearby.

Several men walked along in single file, talking and making notes. None of them had looked up. When Tim spoke they glanced around, startled.

"Good morning, gentlemen. Looks like the weather's holding nicely, wouldn't you say?"

"What the—?"

"Who the hell—?"

"Say, what's—"

"Perhaps you aren't aware of it, but you're trespassing on private property. Some people get a little touchy about their gold mines even when the mines aren't operational."

One of the men stepped forward, pulling his hard hat off his head. "There's obviously some mistake here. We have written instructions from the owner giving us permission to be here. We've been in and out of here several times in the past few weeks. Nobody's said anything."

"And just who gave you this permission?"

The man flipped open a metal-bound notebook and shuffled through the papers. He lifted one, squinting at the signature. "Jason Barringer," he read.

"Mr. Barringer has never owned this property and has no authority to give anyone permission to be here."

"Now wait a minute. I don't know what's going on here but I have my instructions." The man glanced at the others and they moved over so they stood in a V. "I don't know who you are, mister, but you aren't going to start handing out any orders around here."

Tim turned his head slightly, his gaze resting on Sam, who stood out of sight of the other men. Tim nodded. The small group standing in front of the mine looked astonished as several men carrying rifles materialized around them.

Pleasantly, Tim said, "I'm sure the sheriff would like to have the opportunity to meet with all of you and have a little chat. He's been having some problems in the area lately with unauthorized entry, stolen cattle, that sort of thing. No doubt he'd be interested in discussing the matter with you."

The men with the hard hats looked at each other, then at their spokesman and, without waiting for instructions, headed toward their trucks.

"Look, I don't want any trouble," the man began.

"Neither do we. If you'll come with us, I think we can get this matter settled to the satisfaction of all concerned."

Sam pulled up at that moment in the Jeep. Tim motioned for the man to get in next to Sam. Then Tim and Greg got in behind him.

They began the trek to town. "I don't understand what's going on," the engineer said, shaking his head in bewilderment.

Tim replied, "That's all right. You will soon enough."

Elisabeth came awake with a sudden jerk, then realized she had only been dreaming. The bedroom was filled with bright morning sunshine, and she knew she must have overslept.

She rolled over and stared at the place where Tim had been earlier, remembering what had happened the night before. She groaned and buried her head in the pillow. That man had the power to turn her brain into mush by doing no more than holding her. Every time he kissed her, her body turned to gelatin.

Her first mistake had been to think she could continue to sleep beside him after lying to him about the nature of their marriage. Just because he didn't remember those two weeks didn't mean that she could ignore what had taken place between them. But when the unexpected chance to gain some control over the situation had come her way, she grabbed it. What she hadn't taken into account was that she would betray herself.

Elisabeth crawled out of bed and padded into the shower. How could she possibly hope to think clearly as long as she was in his presence daily and shared his bed every night? Why was she so weak that she couldn't find the self-discipline to move her things into another room, insist that the marriage had served its purpose and get on with her life?

Her love for her husband had captured her as surely as if he'd wrapped her in thick bonds that could not be loosened.

After she dressed, Elisabeth wandered down to the kitchen and made some toast, poured a cup of coffee and stood there munching on her breakfast while daydreaming about Tim.

She would never forget their wedding day.

Her grandfather had been so pleased. Tim had been laughing, teasing the nurses, thanking the judge, and she had stood there watching the scene, convinced she was out of her mind.

Ever since she'd first seen Tim, she had been acting out of character. When had she ever been so biddable, so agreeable...so enamored? .

Because they hadn't wanted to be gone far from the hospital, Tim suggested they take a ride, maybe find a decent-looking restaurant and have something to eat, then go back to the homestead.

Once again she had allowed him to take control of the situation. He'd acted so relaxed, as though getting married was nothing new to him.

Elisabeth glanced around the kitchen, disoriented for a moment because she'd been so caught up in her memories. Rinsing her cup, she decided to go upstairs to write in hopes of getting her mind off Tim.

She no sooner sat down in her chair when her memories resumed...

"I suppose we should tell Mrs. Brodie," Tim had said as he held the car door open for her to step out. "Otherwise, she might have an attack of some sort when I follow you into your bedroom tonight."

Elisabeth could feel herself blushing and hated the ridiculous betrayal of nerves. His grin became a chuckle when he saw the look on her face.

"Uh, look, Tim. We should think about this before doing anything hasty."

"Well, you know her heart better than I do. If you think she can handle the shock..." He left the sentence hanging, took her hand and began to draw her to the front steps.

"No, about sleeping in my bedroom," she blurted out.

He stopped in his tracks. Turning her to face him, he said, "There's surely no question about that, is there?"

She stood looking at him, unable to respond.

"Wait a minute. Are you under some kind of crazy impression that I married you because of Charlie?"

"It's just that we don't know each other very well and—"

"Exactly. But we have the rest of our lives to get acquainted, and I want to do it sleeping next to you every night."

Why was she protesting, she wondered. Who did she think she was kidding? She hadn't been able to sleep the night before, just knowing that he was down the hallway from her. The kiss they had shared that first evening had awakened something inside her that refused to go back to sleep.

He had never given any intimation that he would treat the marriage as one without conjugal rights.

Whether to tell Mrs. Brodie or not was not tested because she wasn't in evidence when they went in. Tim quietly followed Elisabeth into her room. He looked around with an interested gaze, then walked over to the bed that took up almost one entire wall of the room.

"My God. What's this?"

She laughed. She couldn't help it. "My grandfather found that somewhere and carried it home to surprise me one year right after I went away to school. The original hangings were rotten so he had new ones made with matching covers. He said it's several hundred years old and was brought to America from somewhere in Europe." She walked over and touched one of the drapes. "He's convinced some king slept in it."

Tim walked around it, eyeing the platform on which it stood. There were steps on either side to get up to it.

"It's big enough to hold a dozen kings. Don't you get lost in it?"

She smiled. "I've grown used to it. He had a mattress custom made. It's very comfortable." She leaned against one of the four posters and watched as he wandered around the room, picking up ornaments and studying them, then replacing them. It suddenly occurred to her that he was nervous. Perhaps as nervous as she was. Not that that was possible. No doubt he had shared a bed before, while she had always slept alone.

Elisabeth wished she had more experience. She had always been aloof from boys her own age, wary of becoming too friendly. Her mother had cautioned her about encouraging someone if she weren't careful. So she had been very careful. She would scarcely exchange a word with a boy.

Her classmates would laugh to see her now. She had been the young woman in college who never dated, who spent all her time studying or writing, who knew so little about men. And she had married a man she had just met.

Abruptly Elisabeth turned and went into the bathroom and closed the door. She was trembling so hard she thought her knees were going to buckle. Glancing into the mirror, a white-faced woman stared back at her with large, shadowed eyes.

How ridiculous. She was acting like one of the wimpy virgin heroines in one of her historical novels. What was she expecting him to do, attack her? She smiled, trying to picture Tim in a scene from one of her books.

No doubt her editor would be amazed to discover that all those sensuous love scenes had been taken completely from Elisabeth's fertile imagination. Since she'd been an apt student she fully understood human anatomy and related subjects. But none of that knowledge helped her to deal with her emotions at the moment.

She felt as though she had to walk into a classroom for a final exam without having studied for it. She had no idea what would happen to her if she were to flunk. Take the course over? What if she couldn't learn? Had no aptitude?

What a silly twit she was being. With jerky movements she pulled her clothes off and got into the shower. The soothing spray caused her to relax somewhat, and by the time she stepped out, she was able to see her situation in a lighter vein.

All she had to do was to explain to Tim that— Well, she could just say that she had never— Then again, she could keep her mouth shut and let him find out on his own.

The coward's way, perhaps, but better than stammering her way through a ridiculous confession. Elisabeth reached for her gown, which hung on the back of the door, and slipped it over her head.

She eyed her reflection in the mirror. The hot spray had warmed her, given her cheeks more color and caused her hair to form wispy curls around her face. She shook her head. She couldn't hide in here all night, she decided firmly. Lifting her chin slightly and filled with conscious resolve, she opened the door and strode into the other room . . . only to find Tim lying across the bed asleep.

Elisabeth almost burst out laughing at the difference between her imaginings and reality. He had probably gotten tired of waiting for her and had stretched out to become more comfortable. He'd removed his suit jacket, his socks and shoes, and unbuttoned his shirt.

Moving carefully so she wouldn't disturb him, she crept up on the bed and scooted over, giving him plenty of room. She'd left the bathroom light on for him and now wasn't sure whether she should turn it off or leave it. Since turning it off would mean that she had to get up again, she chose the easier course.

She slowly stretched out on the bed, determined to allow him to rest, and bit her lip to keep from laughing. Her eager bridegroom must not have gotten any more sleep the night before than she did.

Elisabeth didn't remember going to sleep, but she definitely remembered waking up. Tim was kissing her, touching her, murmuring to her, and she felt as though her skin was on fire everywhere he touched her.

"So sweet," he murmured, "so lusciously scented and sweet."

Sometime in the night he had obviously come awake enough to get undressed. There was no doubt in Elisabeth's mind that he had not bothered with pajamas.

He tugged at her gown, sliding the thin straps off her shoulders and shimmying it down her body until she was as bare as he.

Elisabeth would never forget that beautiful night when Tim had initiated her into the rites of lovemaking with all the painstaking skill at his disposal. How had he known that she had been frightened and had needed some time? By allowing her a chance to relax and fall asleep Tim had insured that she never regained her stiff uncertainty, which might have contributed to her discomfort. His tender caresses gently led her from one plateau of arousal to the next. When she hesitantly imitated his caresses he gave her whispered encouragements in his passion-roughened voice.

By the time he took her she was as eager as he to move to this next joyous step of sharing. How could she have known what beauty there was to be given in such a manner?

He taught her about her own body and its secret responses. During the following days they had spent their time with her grandfather, their nights in each other's arms.

Until the day they quarreled...the day he was hurt.

Chapter Ten

Looking back, Elisabeth knew the quarrel had been silly, but it had been further evidence that she was losing control over her life...all parts of her life, even her professional one.

She had gone into her office looking for something without a thought as to how revealing it would be to Tim, a man who obviously missed very little.

He'd walked in without her hearing him until he spoke. "Who is Lisa Barry?"

She froze in her task of looking through her top desk drawer, then slowly turned around. He was holding an award that had come in the mail a few days before. She had opened it, glanced at it then tossed it aside. Lisa Barry was not on her list of priorities at the time.

He was reading the certificate. Lisa Barry had won the nomination for best historical writer of the year, an award given by a prestigious national publishing magazine.

"I am," she said evenly, despite the fact that her heart was pounding in her chest like cannons going off for a twenty-one-gun salute.

He glanced around then, taking in the reference books, the computer, several shelves that included her books. He walked over and touched each one.

"You've written eight novels."

She nodded.

"Charlie thought you'd only sold one."

"I know."

He tapped his finger against the shelves. "Does he know about these?"

She shook her head.

"Why not?"

She couldn't answer the question. Was it because she had been afraid Charlie would make fun of her? Because she had enjoyed not sharing her secret life, not even with her grandfather? Because—

"I saw no reason to tell him."

Tim turned and looked at her, and the expression in his eyes caught her off guard. She had never seen him look that way. A frisson of fear ran up and down her arms.

"So you have kept the information that you are a published, award-winning author from not only me, your husband, but your grandfather, the person you reputedly love more than anyone in the world? What other secrets do you keep locked inside that private little head, I wonder?"

"I don't see that it's anyone's business whether I'm published or not. Granddad knows I write. He wouldn't care about the kinds of things I write about."

Tim leaned against the doorjamb and studied her as though he'd never seen her before, as though he wasn't too sure he liked what he saw.

"No doubt you've had a good reason for building the walls you carry around with you. Perhaps they've helped you to survive this far. But to keep your grandfather in the dark about something like this is the height of selfishness. The man is so damned proud of you that he glows at the mention of your name. He would have enjoyed every single moment of each book, from manuscript to publication, but you're so damned afraid to let anyone see you're human, that you struggle and worry, that you have moments of doubt and despair, you've bottled up everything that makes you a real person. All any of us are left with are the careful reflections of who you want us to see."

He straightened. "I feel sorry for you, Elisabeth. You're hurting yourself much more than you've hurt Charlie." He took a step back so he was in the hallway. "Forgive me for trespassing in your private domain. You may be sure I won't do it again."

He strode away, leaving her standing there staring at him.

Hours later she found out that he had gone riding. Then his horse had returned without him.

A light tap on her office door brought Elisabeth out of her reverie. Since Mrs. Brodie never bothered her in the office, she knew who had tapped. She quickly moved to the door and opened it. Before she could say anything, Tim spoke.

"I'm sorry for bothering you when you're writing. I just wanted to let you know that Greg and I are leaving for Denver. I'm not sure how long I'll be gone. It may be a few days."

She could only stare at him in shock, her mind still caught up in the whirling memories of the last few weeks. "You're leaving?" she finally repeated.

He leaned down and gave her a brief but thorough kiss. "Yes. But I'll be back. We have to talk."

With that he spun on his heel and strode away, disappearing down the stairway at the front of the house. She stood there as though paralyzed. Where was he going and why? She hadn't said goodbye to Greg but maybe he, too, would be back.

Yes. They had to talk. Somehow she had to come to terms with her feelings and her fears. She had used Tim's memory lapse to try to run away, at least emotionally, from what they shared, but her continued responses to his lovemaking made a mockery of her efforts.

As much as she loved him, did she have the courage to remove her walls and allow herself to be vulnerable? Could she survive?

The question had now become: could she survive without him? Elisabeth had a strong hunch that she didn't want to test herself. Not now.

Tim and Greg drove to Denver, stopping at Tim's place long enough for him to pack a few items of clothing he had not taken to Cripple Creek with him. Then they drove to the airport and caught an evening flight to New York.

After landing at La Guardia, they directed the cab driver to the hotel where Tim had made reservations. Since both of them knew the plan, there had been little conversation during their travels.

Crawling into bed that night Tim had a fleeting thought that he would be sleeping alone for the first time in almost a month. He had already grown accustomed to finding Elisabeth next to him. He lay there, staring into the dark, going over the surge of memories that had been flooding his mind during the day.

She had lied to him about their relationship. He realized that now. He remembered with great clarity their first night together and how nervous she had been. Their long drive had done little to relax her, and by the time they had reached her bedroom she had been trembling with anxiety. He had known then that he couldn't force her into a relationship she wasn't ready for.

He had waited for her to come out of the bathroom to tell her, reminding himself to have the patience to take it one step at a time. Eventually he stretched out across the bed. At least they were married, he remembered thinking. No longer did he have to sleep down the hallway from her. The important thing was that they were together.

Tim had felt like a fool when he woke up and discovered that he had drifted off to sleep. She was asleep. He had gotten up and taken a shower, then crawled into bed beside her. Thinking to give her a soft kiss good night he had moved closer to her. His kiss lingered, and his hand lightly brushed against her.

She had turned toward him, relaxed and at ease. Would he ever forget that night or the nights that followed?

Why had she lied about those days and nights spent loving each other, growing increasingly close?

Had she still been angry because he had found out her closely guarded secret, the existence of Lisa Barry? Yes, he'd been upset with her attitude and he had let her know it. His impatience had gotten the better of him. Why did she have to be so guarded with everyone, including the people who loved her?

Hadn't she understood why he'd been so upset? If she was still keeping her grandfather at a distance after all these years, where did that leave her new husband?

He had several questions for her, but first he wanted to deal with Jason Barringer. Whatever happened between him and Elisabeth, Tim wanted to know that she would be left in peace by the other members of the family. This trip to New York should take care of Charlie's wishes. After that, Tim intended to deal with his own.

He shifted in bed, turning on his side. Tim realized that he was looking forward to the meeting tomorrow. He smiled and drifted off to sleep.

The next morning Tim and Greg stepped out of the taxi that had brought them to the Wall Street address from their mid-town Manhattan hotel. The imposing edifice standing before them towered high above them, its marble walls attesting to several generations of money that had married and intermingled to produce the man they had flown halfway across the continent to see.

Tim looked at Greg and they exchanged a smile that boded ill to someone, then walked to the entrance.

After being questioned at several different levels, the two men were finally ushered into the executive offices, Jason's lair, high above the clouds. From the size of the waiting area that greeted them as they stepped off the elevators, and from the ornate furnishings, Tim recognized the subtle intimidation inherent in everything they came across.

At long last they were directed to Jason's administrative assistant. The man rose from behind his desk and came around to greet them. Tim knew what the assistant saw—two men in expensive, conservative suits with an air of quiet power and determination.

"May I be of some assistance to you, gentlemen?" the young man asked with a smile.

Since Tim knew that the man had already been notified of their presence in the building and their desire to see Jason Barringer, the question was prompted by curiosity more than politeness.

"We'd like to see Mr. Barringer."

The young man's head was nodding before Tim finished speaking. "Yes, sir. That's what I understand. However, it seems that you neglected to call first for an appointment. Had you called, I could have explained that Mr. Barringer is tied up in meetings and won't be available all day." He turned and looked at an appointment calendar on his desk. "Perhaps you could return—"

"Oh, that won't be necessary." Tim opened his briefcase and pulled out a large manila envelope and handed it to the man. "Just tell him that his brother-in-law brought these for him."

For a moment the man looked startled, then he quickly resumed his blank expression.

Tim gestured to the comfortable-looking chairs opposite the large desk. "We'll be right here should he change his mind about seeing us."

Tim and Greg sat while the young man warily watched them. Glancing at the double doors on the other side of the desk, the man must have made up his mind to follow Tim's instructions rather than take a chance on misunderstanding the situation. He nodded and disappeared behind the doors.

Tim and Greg refused to meet each other's gaze. Instead, they reached for a couple of magazines in unison and began to flip through them.

The man soon reappeared.

"Mr. Barringer can see you now."

Tim nodded. He and Greg walked through the door the young man held open, then paused inside the room until the door closed behind them.

The room appeared to be large enough to hold a basketball court. Light flooded through the eastern wall that was made entirely of glass, as was the south wall. The desk could have been used for a game of table tennis.

As they walked toward the desk, the man seated behind it watched them without rising. They did not stop until they reached the edge of the desk. Then they stood waiting.

Jason took in Tim's apparel, then turned his gaze to Greg. He glanced at the manila folder in front of him and flicked his finger against it.

"Care to tell me what this is all about?"

"You wanted to know about the potential of the gold mine on the homestead property. I decided if you were so willing to spend your own money to find out, the least I could do was see that you got the information as quickly as I did."

"What's the meaning of the statement signed by the engineer?"

"Oh, that. Well, the sheriff wanted to get all the facts clear on what was going on. The engineer was very obliging, as you can see."

Once more Jason looked at Greg. "I don't believe we've met."

Tim spoke up. "This is Gregory Duncan, my attorney."

Jason's brows went up. "What happened to Neil?"

"He's Charlie's attorney."

"I see." Jason made a steeple of his fingers. "What do you want from me?"

"I want you to leave Elisabeth alone. You have your empire, you and Marcus. You've never shown any interest in the Colorado property before. It was never yours. It belongs to her now because Charlie wanted her to have it."

"According to these reports, the mine looks promising."

"Yes, it does. I intend to tell Elisabeth that you and Marcus had the preliminary work done as a wedding gift for us." He smiled. "For which we thank you very much. It was a very generous gesture on your part."

"I don't need to ask what's in this for you."

Tim met his gaze with a level one of his own. "Given your perspective about life, I'm sure you think you have all the answers. There is one thing I feel I should mention, though."

"And that is?"

"For some reason Charlie didn't like you, Jason, grandson or not. Perhaps it had something to do with the dossier he kept on both you and Marcus over the years, a detailed account of your business practices, many of which would prove to be interesting reading material to the IRS."

Jason straightened in his chair and leaned forward, but he didn't say a word.

"Charlie felt that once he was gone you and Marcus might try some of your tactics to convince Elisabeth to leave the ranch. He knew how much you enjoy intimidating people. If there's one thing you enjoy more than money, it's power. Charlie understood that very well."

"You can't prove a thing. Our business practices are perfectly legal."

"Of course they are. But you know how it is. Once the IRS starts nosing around a company they tend to watch it a great deal more closely, scrutinizing, auditing. So many decisions are left to their discretion— interpretation of the statutes, that sort of thing. They can stick with you closer than a cocklebur and can be just as hard to get away from."

"Are you threatening me?"

"Why should I do that? We understand each other, just as Charlie understood you and me. He passed me those dossiers in case they were needed. I promised to guard them carefully."

"You son of a—"

"Ah, ah. Name calling is so juvenile, don't you agree? We're grown men...relatives, actually. No reason we can't get along."

Tim nodded toward the papers. "Those are your copies to keep. We have the originals. If we should have any reason to think you or Marcus are behind any problems that might occur around the mine or the ranch, Mr. Duncan will be in touch with you."

Jason stood. "Now, wait a minute. We can't be blamed for everything that might happen out there, for God's sake."

"Of course you can't. Just as we certainly can't be held responsible if the IRS suddenly begins to take an intense interest in your many businesses." Tim spread his hands. "Things happen. All part of life."

He and Greg walked out of the room, into the lobby, into the elevator, through the echoing marble lobby on the ground floor and out to the street.

Tim took a deep breath and sighed. "Ah, smell that fresh diesel and soot-filled air. A welcome relief to the rather closed atmosphere we just left, wouldn't you say?"

Greg lifted his brow. "I got a distinct scent of fear upstairs."

"Not surprising."

"So that takes care of Mr. Barringer."

"I think so, and so did Charlie. I think Jason will take into consideration the possible consequences of going after Elisabeth, and decide that it isn't worth the risk."

"I don't think the man knew what hit him."

"That's the point. Nothing's hit him, yet. Charlie wanted to give him fair warning. If the man behaves himself, he'll be home free."

"If he gets vindictive, he'll—"

"Find out a little more about the uses of power."

A cab pulled up and they got in and headed uptown.

Greg dropped Tim off at the homestead but refused his offer to spend the night. He wanted to put in a few hours on the road to Missouri so he would be home by the next day.

Tim didn't insist. He had other things on his mind. He let himself into the house and looked around.

This house would always remind Tim of Charlie. He could almost hear Charlie's voice from the other room, smell the scent of the cigars he'd smoked until the doctors had insisted he give them up. He would miss the old man. He just hoped he had carried out his instructions in a way that would have pleased him.

Carrying his bag, Tim started up the stairs. He decided to shower and change before dinner. He was tired. He'd done a great deal of traveling in the past couple of days. Plus he had a feeling of letdown, which was not unusual. He generally experienced the feeling whenever he finished an assignment.

The water felt good beating down on his shoulders. He stood there for a long time, allowing his mind to stay blank. He didn't want to think about the next few hours and how important they would be to his future.

When he walked into the bedroom he glanced at the bed. Never had it seemed so inviting to him. Slowly he walked over to it. Climbing the stairs, he decided to relax for a few minutes. He still had plenty of time before dinner. He'd just stretch out for a while, then get dressed and go find Elisabeth.

Those were his last thoughts before he fell sound asleep.

Chapter Eleven

Tim was awakened by a lingering kiss. He opened his eyes and saw a green-eyed young woman with moonlight-tipped blond hair staring at him. Her hair fell around them like a silken veil, enclosing them in a scented haven.

"I've invented a new fairy tale," she whispered with a smile. "The sleeping prince, found in all his natural splendor, adorned only by the soft shadows of early evening, awaiting the touch of one special person to arouse him from his slumber."

Tim slipped his arms around her, making sure he wasn't still asleep. She felt very real in his arms. "You'd better kiss me again. I may still be dreaming."

Elisabeth searched for and found his mouth once more. This time Tim took control, threading his hand through her hair, his fingers splayed against the back of her head. With possessive insistence he explored her mouth with his tongue, delicately probing. She met his thrust with a dainty, duel-like rhythm of her own.

When the kiss ended they were both breathless.

"If I'd known I was going to be greeted with such an enthusiastic welcome I might have considered leaving before now." Tim began to stroke her back, wishing she wasn't wearing so many clothes.

"You've missed the point," she said with an impish grin, running her finger along his jawline.

"Which is?"

"I'm trying to bewitch you so you won't ever want to leave me again."

Tim's hand stilled at the words. "You are?"

She nodded her head emphatically.

With an unexpected move he rolled until she was lying beneath him. He propped himself up on his elbows and stared at her. She gazed at him with a serene air he wasn't sure he'd ever seen before.

"You mean all those hours of careful preparation I've spent listing the reasons we should stay together were unnecessary? All my arguments, my most persuasive manner, my unassailable charm aren't going to be called upon to convince you?"

"You sound disappointed," she pointed out dryly.

He laughed. "Not on your life. I'm relieved, even if I don't understand."

"Don't you? Then you underestimate your own charm."

"None of my friends would agree with you, believe me."

Elisabeth placed her hand along his jawline. "I love you, Tim."

Her words jolted him as though he'd received an electric shock. He could feel his heart racing so fast he wondered if it was going to spin out of control.

"When did you discover that?"

She cocked her head, as though in deep thought. "Oh, a few hours after I walked into Granddad's room and saw you standing there for the first time."

"That soon?"

"That soon. We were sitting together on the sofa in front of the fireplace. You were talking and I was watching you and I realized that now I understood why my mother had chosen to spend her life with my father, despite everything that stood between them."

"So when I suggested that we marry, you agreed because..."

"Because I had no other choice, feeling the way I did."

He rewarded her for her honesty by giving her a very thorough kiss. When he raised his head he was frowning slightly. "Then why did you lie?"

"About what?"

"When I had my memory lapse. Why did you want me to believe that ours was just a pretend marriage?"

Her cheeks pinkened. "You remember differently?"

"Yes. I remember everything that happened between the two of us. No wonder I found myself making love to you in my sleep. No wonder it felt so natural. We had already been together so often. So why lie?"

"I think that at some deep level I don't fully understand, I was trying to protect myself from being hurt. Before I met you, my life had been carefully controlled and choreographed. I was in charge. I knew what I wanted in life, or thought I did—a sense of safety, a haven, a place where I'd be without pain."

"Cemeteries offer such a place, you know."

She reached up and nipped his ear. "Meeting you put me in a tailspin. You didn't give me time to think, to gain control, before we were married and caught up in the whirlwind of our desire for each other."

"And you didn't like that?"

"I was afraid of it. Your losing your memory gave me an opportunity to regroup, to try to regain my sense of self, to come to terms with everything that had happened and to apply some logic to the situation." She ran her fingers along his collarbone, then made a trail across his chest. "Besides, I wanted to give you an out."

"Me? What are you talking about?"

"You were so shocked to see me when you woke up that morning, don't you remember? As though you couldn't conceive of a reason you would wake up in my bed. I felt as though I was seeing the real Tim Walker for the first time, not the man I'd married and been living with. I was getting a true reaction from you because you no longer remembered any promises you might have made to Charlie."

He groaned. "I never made any promises to Charlie where you were concerned."

"You told him you would protect me. That you would take care of me."

"Of course I did. You were my wife when I told him that. I suppose I assumed that you would also protect and take care of me, as well." He touched the back of his head where he'd been hit. "Which you did."

"I just didn't want you to feel obligated to me, that's all. Particularly if you couldn't even remember who I was. I thought if your memory didn't return you would feel free to leave without any complication."

He cupped her breast and gently massaged it. "Do you consider yourself a complication?"

"I didn't want to be." She shifted slightly, moving her legs so he lay between them. "Granddad told me that you never stayed in one place too long and that I would be taking advantage of you if I tied you down and took away your freedom."

"Oh, he did, did he?"

She nodded.

"Maybe I'm ready to be tied down, as you call it. Freedom isn't all it's cracked up to be. I know what it's like to be somewhere and realize that nobody knows...or cares...where you are. There's your ultimate freedom. It's a cold and lonely place, and frankly I'm tired of it. I can think of nothing nicer than to discover that my whereabouts are important to somebody, that there's someone somewhere who is thinking about me, concerned about me, maybe even a little worried if they haven't heard from me."

"Does that mean you're going to stay here with me and not go running off without any explanation like you just did?"

He grinned. "Well, you have to give me a little time to adjust to my new status in life. I'm not going to be able to change overnight."

"Are you going to tell me where you've been?"

He leaned down until his lips were only a fraction of an inch away from hers. "I might be persuaded to talk if I were given the proper incentive."

She raised her head to kiss him, then with a sudden lunge pushed him off balance so he fell back while she scrambled off the bed.

"What was that for?" he asked in an aggrieved tone.

She glanced over her shoulder at him. "You're much too eager to be coaxed, my friend. Besides, our dinner is getting cold."

"How can you think about food at a time like this?" He sat up, pushing his hand through his hair. He was thoroughly aroused, and since he was as bare as the day he was born, his condition could not be overlooked.

Elisabeth was thinking the same thing, but she had scarcely eaten since he'd been gone, and she had to eat now. Besides, Mrs. Brodie would be pulling her hair, trying to keep their meal edible.

She picked up a pair of his jeans and tossed them to him with a grin. "I'll see you downstairs."

Elisabeth waited until halfway through their meal before she brought up the argument they'd had about her career the day he was hurt.

"You mean the discussion we had about your alter ego, Lisa Barry?" he asked.

"Yes. I felt guilty about your being hurt, as though somehow I was at fault because we had argued earlier—" He shook his head at her fractured logic, but she continued. "I also felt a little guilty about telling you our marriage was just pretence—"

"Now that was a totally justified guilt."

"Before Granddad died I finally told him about Lisa Barry and asked his forgiveness for not sharing her with him."

He took her hand. "I'm glad. He deserved to know."

"Yes. I felt very ashamed of myself because he was so pleased for me... surprised, of course... but his pride was apparent. I'm glad you goaded me into telling him before it was too late."

"I am, too."

She studied the man across from her for a moment before she said, "Having you come into my life blasted so many of my ideas and beliefs about myself. It was as though I was really looking at myself for the first time, and not really liking what I saw."

Tim glanced at her plate. "Are you through eating?"

She looked down, surprised to see that her plate was clean. "Why, yes, I suppose I am."

"Good." He pushed away from the table, took her hand and led her out of the dining room. Instead of crossing the foyer to the front room for coffee, he turned toward the stairway.

"Tim, it's not even eight o'clock yet."

"I don't care. I have this very sudden urge to get horizontal. I can't quite remember why. Maybe my memory's slipping again. Perhaps you'd better come with me and make sure I'm all right.''

She shook her head and with a chuckle followed him up the stairway.

Come to think of it, she realized, he had never told her where he and Greg had gone, or why. Maybe she would test her persuasive powers and see how potent they were.

Elisabeth smiled. Perhaps she had found a new career. Being married to Tim would certainly be entertaining and educational. With a protective movement across her stomach she mentally added, *And probably broadening.*

Epilogue

From her vantage point atop a small rise, Elisabeth viewed the never-ending beauty of the mountains that surrounded her home. This little knoll had always been a favorite place for her to come whenever she wanted to be alone with her thoughts for a while.

Today was one of those days.

Bright wildflowers splashed brilliant color across the meadow, and the green of the aspen and birch trees added richness to the scenic panorama spread before her.

She glanced at the envelope she held in her hand. Elisabeth had lost count of the number of times she had read the letter it contained, her last message from her grandfather. Today, the first anniversary of his death, seemed an appropriate time to bring it out once more, as though in some way she could share the serenity and the beauty of the place with him.

The stationery crackled as she removed the expensive sheets of paper from the envelope and stared at the distinctive handwriting that belied his years. He had written it on her wedding day, but had waited until he was gone to have it given to her.

She began to read.

My darling Elisabeth,

Words cannot begin to express the joy I felt today as I gave you in marriage to such a fine young man as Tim Walker. In the years that I have known him, he has impressed me with his quiet integrity, his determination and plain common sense. I had hoped that someday you would find a man worthy of all you have to offer. It is my belief that you have found him. Thank God he immediately recognized and appreciated you for who and what you are . . . a very special person.

I can rest easy now, knowing that Tim will always be there for you. I know what you told me about not wanting the ranch given to you, so I know you are going to be upset with me when Neil reads the will. Please hear me out before you make any decisions.

Despite all that I have ever accumulated in this life, the homestead has always been where my heart resides. I was born there, all my roots are there, and I would like to think that you and your children will continue to live there down through the years. I have made the necessary arrangements to see that you are given no trouble over this inheritance, and I trust Tim to take care of any unpleasantness that might occur. I know I can count on him to keep both of you safe and secure.

I have always felt that God understood my loneliness, so He sent you to me to add meaning to my life. I always regretted that your father never knew you, and if there's anything to what the churches say about an afterlife, I know that he was pleased I managed to find you and bring you home where you belong.

The only request that I leave with you is to be happy in your newfound love. Give of yourself, for if you do, you will discover as I did that no matter how much you give, you seem to receive double and triple the amount in return. Never be afraid of loving, no matter what happens. Love is what makes everything else in your life worthwhile.

Your loving grandfather

There was a slight sound from somewhere behind her, a rustling of the thick blades of tall grass. She hastily wiped the moisture from her eyes before glancing around. Her eyes lit and she watched Tim striding up the hillside toward her, a baby tucked comfortably into the curve of his arm.

His smile became a laughing grin when he saw her face turned toward him. "Hello, darling. I wouldn't have disturbed you except your daughter can't tell time. I've been trying to explain that she couldn't be hungry yet, that she only ate a short while ago. But she's as stubborn as her mother and refuses to listen to reason."

He leaned over and carefully placed the baby in Elisabeth's arms before sprawling alongside her in the grass.

Young Jessica left no doubt in anyone's mind what she expected, no, insisted, on having, and Elisabeth unbuttoned her blouse and brought the tiny infant to her breast. Jessica's fretful cry was cut off in mid-sound, and she began to noisily enjoy her meal.

"What a little pig," Elisabeth muttered with a sigh. "I have trouble picturing us ever making a lady out of her. She wants what she wants when she wants it."

Tim cupped her other breast. "I don't see anything wrong with that philosophy. It's always worked very well for me."

She leaned toward him and gave him a brief kiss, which he returned with enthusiasm. When their lips parted Tim leaned back so Elisabeth could lean against him.

"What a beautiful spot. No wonder you enjoy coming up here."

"Yes. Granddad and I used to come up here and have picnics during the summers I was home. He said he always felt like a king sitting here, the master of all he surveyed."

Tim glanced down and saw the letter lying beside her. He recognized it as the one Neil had given her the day of her grandfather's funeral. She had waited until Jessica's birth to give it to him to read. He had been touched by the sensitivity she had shown in giving it to him then, at a time when he'd felt so inadequate to be all the things Jessica needed in a father.

Charlie had believed in him and Charlie had been an excellent judge of character. He had seen something in Tim that Tim himself wasn't sure existed. All Tim knew was that he would do the best he could to provide the safety and security Elisabeth and Jessica, and any other children they might have, deserved.

He watched his young daughter greedily clutch her mother's breast and smiled, understanding and appreciating her greed.

Elisabeth was his love, even when he hadn't remembered all that they had shared. Somewhere deep inside he had known and recognized her importance in his life and her place in his heart, a love never to be forgotten.

*   *   *   *   *

Silhouette **Romance** ®

COMING NEXT MONTH

#682 RUN, ISABELLA—Suzanne Carey
Isabel Sloan had granted her father's last wish and married his handsome protégé, Max Darien. But did her new husband want her—or her father's legacy?

#683 THE PERFECT WIFE—Marcine Smith
Nona Alexander's first marriage had convinced her she wasn't meant for wedded bliss. But Nicholas Kendrick's ardent pursuit was quickly changing her mind!

#684 SWEET PROTECTOR—Patricia Ellis
Melanie Rogers saved Mac Chandler from kidnappers, nursed him to health and helped him solve a mystery. But once all the excitement settled down, would he follow suit?

#685 THIEF OF HEARTS—Beverly Terry
Tara Linton had unwittingly crossed paths with bumbling jewel thieves. Investigator Sam Miller made it his duty to protect her—and got his heart stolen right from under his nose!

#686 MOTHER FOR HIRE—Marie Ferrarella
Widower Bryan Marlowe knew that only a woman's touch could calm down his four mischievous sons, but new nanny Kate Llewellyn was wreaking havoc—on his heart....

#687 FINALLY HOME—Arlene James
Nicky Collier was chasing corporate secrets, and instead uncovered a love sweeter than she'd ever dreamed possible. Could she convince Gage Bardeen that she'd found what she'd really been looking for?

AVAILABLE THIS MONTH: